BURN THE SAME

BURN THE SAME

THE BURNER TRILOGY
BOOK ONE

MARIANNA PALMER

THE BURNER TRILOGY

Burn the Same

Alternate Burn

Burnout

Red Empress Publishing
www.RedEmpressPublishing.com

Cover Design by Cherith Vaughan
https://www.facebook.com/coversbycherith

This is for my sister, Esther, my best friend, my first reader and constant support. Without her, any book I write would be trashed before going anywhere.
Thank you!

CHAPTER 1

$\mathcal{I}$ce and fire are complete opposites, and yet they burn the same way. Both are beautiful, and both are deadly. This was the first coherent thought I ever had when I was about the age of three. And when I realized my skin wasn't just cold, it was ice, I had to accept that I could be both beautiful and deadly.

It didn't get any easier when I met Fire.

As I traveled on the fastest train out of town, the first part of my journey north that would end in Washington State, my mind was focused on my first thought and wondered what my last one would be when I inevitably stopped running. I gripped my hands together, too hot and confined in their gloved prison. I really hoped the trio that had just boarded the train would get off at the next stop. I knew they were Breathers. If I survived this, I'd be sure to make an entry about them in my ever-growing notebooks.

I had been on the run since I was six, when my parents had sold me out. The day I started my diaries. The day I learned it was a certain death to trust any living thing.

Once again, I swallowed the dirty and dry lump in my

throat. *It's alright, Laoni,* I told myself. The Breathers could only sense that *someone* like me was on the train, but they wouldn't be able to pinpoint who. I wore the most unassuming outfit I could imagine, a dirty, off-white rain jacket two sizes too big, which let its gigantic hood fall over my face. I chose it for two reasons: one, it was so big, it covered my face so no one would be distracted and, two, because I felt like an elfin princess with a hood of protective magic around my face.

A perfect disguise.

I bit my lip as outside the winding train, the sun sunk behind the blurred scenery. With the Breathers coming up slowly, like a fog of poisonous gas, I did not want the night's own dread added. Sure, the cold of late fall enhanced my powers, but I never liked the dark.

I felt my breath push against my already parched lips. The Breathers were getting closer. *Please, please, please,* I begged anything that would listen. *Don't let them find me.* I wasn't exactly sure what would happen if they did. I had always run. The fear they spit into the very back of my bones was as instinctual as predator and prey. A deer doesn't know what exactly will happen if a wolf catches it. It just knows not to let it.

I wished I could be sure that all the Breathers would do was eat me if they got me. I felt my heart throw itself against my ribcage, urging me to run. They were next to me.

"Hello, young lady, mind if one of us takes that seat?" The voice of melted silk pouring down my skin urged me to trust him.

I wasn't that stupid. "Go ahead," I said with a soft smile. I sure hoped he wasn't one of the Bloodhounds—he'd hear my heartbeat, feel the rush of my pulse, see past my phony smile. The other two moved on down the train.

"What a night..."

"It's a bit cold." I pulled out my book to hide behind even as I shifted my backpack with all my worldly goods inside onto my back. I was ready to run. But if he'd just leave me alone, I'd…Nope. He was staring at me. He hadn't taken the hint.

"Nice gloves," he noted.

"Cold," I barely whispered out. What could I do? Freeze the glass? Smash out the window? Landing would hurt. Could I jump and run without breaking my legs? Freeze the floor? No, I wasn't powerful enough to ice up the metal to a point where I could break through.

I was trapped. The wolf had me. But I tried to breathe. Maybe, just maybe, he had given up on finding his prey and was just being pleasant to a stranger.

Yeah, and I was a pink raccoon.

"Why don't you take them off?"

I caught a look from the corner of my eyes. The Breather had whitish blonde hair and piercing purple eyes. He saw past everything. His muscles were burly, trained—fit enough to kill.

I didn't answer him. The window it was. I sure hoped I wouldn't break my leg.

Suddenly, the Breather's hand shot out and grabbed mine, holding it in a grip of iron. His other hand pulled my hood down. But then his grip slackened, his mouth gaped. It was nice to know that even the Breathers weren't immune to the beauty that nature had given me. He was caught off guard. Most were, even with the warnings.

The unnatural whiteness to my hair like fresh snow on the first day of winter, my clear and flawless skin, my eyes so blue they shined like an otherworldly light was inside them.

"Yes, I'm beautiful!" I said and pulled free. By moving my arm, I used my power and the window iced over. I kicked it out and jumped. The open air surrounded me as I fell. The wind ripped at my ears, stripping past my head.

I had waited too long. Right as I had made my death-defying escape, the train had rumbled over some bridge or another. This particular bridge had a drop of about one hundred feet, and I felt each one as I hit the water. I plummeted and my powers took over. They took great exception to water. Shards of ice split the open air around.

But I sunk to the bottom.

CHAPTER 2

H i Diary,

This is Laoni Hibiscus Kekoa signing in. This is MY diary. I am six years old. I write now because I can't think. Daddy and Mommy are weird. Miss Darlene said when a thought is too big for my head that I should write it down. Well, I am now. Too many big thoughts. First, I touched the puddle. I only wanted to splash a big, huge gush of water. I got stuck. It froze! Right around my ankle.

Stuff like that never happens to Mom or Dad.

It's magic!

And I should be happier. It's like I'm a snow queen! But, being different is harder than the books say. Daddy doesn't want me touching him. Mommy keeps on making my chores longer. I'm scared. Today some people showed up. They want me. I hate them!

There is one guy. He sits down with Daddy every night. Daddy keeps saying, "I don't know. Losing a daughter...I think more is needed."

I don't know what more is.

Mommy and Daddy are fighting. They have loud voices.

Scream, scream, scream every night. Mom hugs me extra hard when she kisses me goodnight.

The lamp on my bedside is dimming. Mommy and Daddy don't notice. Soon I'll be in the dark.

I can't think! A big thought is squeezing my brain. Wait here, Diary. I'm gonna get some water. Gotta be careful. Mommy doesn't want me out of bed at night.

Okay, back. I've got a glass of water. I heard Daddy yelling at Mommy. Something like, "A million, Cher. A million dollars!"

But don't care. Can't. My stomach hurts. So, testing. Miss Darlene tells me you have to test to be a cientist. Well, I don't know if I want to be a cientist or anything. I think I want to jump out of planes. But I do want to know what happens if I stick my finger in a glass of water.

Test one.

Diary, I can barely write. I got a frozen water circle around my finger. Yikes. I make water freeze.

I wonder when I'll get my crown as snow queen.

CHAPTER 3

I climbed, crawled, swam through the rapidly thickening water. But the deer doesn't get a choice when running for her life.

I gasped in utter shock. It wasn't cold. I never get cold. It was just extremely uncomfortable. And ice though I am, the jagged blades sliced at me. As I desperately tried to avoid the blades that kept shifting toward me, escaping the massive amounts of water around me seemed impossible. Each droplet froze on contact with my skin or clothes, leaving me feeling encased.

Slowly but surely, the entirety of the lake, bay, whatever it was, solidified around me. Once again, I was trapped, but this time by my own power. Story of my life. I shifted and pulled but couldn't get out. I looked up to see the train finishing its rumbling turn around the bridge and then disappearing out of sight. Had the Breathers gone with it?

Oh, no…He had followed me. There he was, standing on the ice, watching my struggle with amusement. How? Could those creatures from the darkness fly?

He caught my eyes as he tested the ice. Slowly but as

surefooted as a mountain goat, he trotted toward me. "You seem surprised. Are you so new at this game you don't know how we operate?"

"You so new that you're distracted by a pretty face?" I asked casually, trying to kick my legs.

"I was a tad distracted, it's true. You have the beauty of ice, but though my soul soars at beauty, my heart beats at victory. And logic tells me, pretty girl, that when I subdue you, I'll have both. I know your name is Laoni. I know all about you. Would you like to know my name?" Though he didn't slip over the smooth ice, he also didn't hurry. He respected his prey as a wolf respected a cornered deer. He knew that, even with all his abilities, trapped prey is still the most dangerous creature one can encounter.

"No." I wriggled. I had to get out of here.

"Digory Kelly. I believe in information, see. I want you to know what's going to happen and why. When I capture you, and I will, you'll at least have knowledge along with defeat."

I wasn't listening. No. Never. But sometimes it was nice when the villain told you why they hated you so much. "And?"

"Your power inside is everything. It can be the future. My girl, you are a Burner. You were born with strange chromosomes that heat up and cool down without causing harm to your cells. That kind of energy is limitless. You know how dependent human beings are on fossil fuels, the thing that will destroy the earth if it continues.

"You and your kind are like living batteries. We can use just one of you to power a neighborhood for a year. At sixteen, the power is the most potent. Waiting any longer or using you before then would be problematic. Too young and your kind meltdown, nuclear style. Too old and the power just fizzes out."

Okay, so he was boring now. They wanted my energy?

That was it? Great. Now I couldn't even say they wanted me to take over the world or something. So mundane!

"Never mind. Don't care." I started to struggle again.

"Let's be reasonable about this, Laoni." He crept ever closer. "I know you'll fight, but you shouldn't. I'll bring you back to a good life. You'll be pampered and spoiled, and maybe you'll even survive the transfer process. It's possible. Not that your choice matters.

"You should just give up, my cold girl. I will follow you to the ends of the earth if you run. I know you're a Burner. I can smell it." His nostrils widened as he breathed in my scent. "You're scared of me. But I can be nice, see."

So, he was a Bloodhound. That explained why his companions hadn't joined him, why he had zeroed in on me while they had moved to the other side of the train.

"I hear your heartbeat as if it were mine. I run along the blood in your veins. I exist in your breaths."

I stared him down. My anger tasted bitter on my tongue. Let him come. I had learned a few tricks. As he drew closer, I suddenly stretched out my hand. "Become a blade!" I yelled to the ice and like a loyal canine it sparked to life, dragging thick and sharp shards out of the frozen bay he walked upon. He twisted to the side, dodging the shards as I finally broke free.

Feeling the ice pushing me up and cutting me at the same time, I struggled to run over the frozen wasteland in front of me. The ice was stretching outward. I needed to get out so the water could return to normal. I had no desire to freeze the fish who would never endure a frozen world.

"Don't run!" the Breather yelled, angry in his struggle. His screams could wake the dead. And as I reached the bank, I realized our struggle had brought someone down to watch us.

And so…I met Fire.

CHAPTER 4

ow I begin a data log of sorts. Before, it was just my diary, but it feels more important than ever to talk about everything I've seen. I'll put in what I can, when I can. Now that there's someone else with me, I don't know how often I'll turn to my notebooks. Then again, now that someone is with me, I may turn to my notebooks more often just to avoid him.

Well, let's start with the beginning.

Breathers are a strange and mysterious set of creatures. Human...They look human. I'm sure they have no soul though. Whether they sold it years ago or were born that way remains a mystery to me. All I know is that there are three categories with three very different sets of abilities. They can all draw in our powers so they don't get hurt. But there are distinctions.

First, there are the Runners. I encounter them the most. They are called Runners because that's what they do. They wouldn't dream of using any mechanical forms of transportation. They just run. They can find their prey better that way. They're fast. Strong. I've seen one lift a car to look for me.

The Bloodhounds are a special kind of Runner. All Breathers can sense out Burners, but Bloodhounds become their prey. And Bloodhounds can get the scent of their prey, which means there's no hiding once they do. They know where their prey is then—anywhere. Well, minus underground and surrounded by water, but I'll get to that later.

On the other end of the spectrum are Riders. They drive black and silver motorcycles and do what they're called: ride across America trying to find people like me. They are fast, intelligent, conniving. A bullet wouldn't graze them. It's them who I constantly avoid. But it is the Bloodhounds that scare me.

And the third kind of Breathers are the Flyers. I haven't had the misfortune to run into them much. And I thank any lucky stars I might have. Let's just say I'll write about the Flyers later. I don't really feel like thinking about the time I did run into one...

Bloodhounds only rarely team up with Riders. As far as I can tell, Burners are a valuable commodity. And that makes it a very competitive sport. But Bloodhounds take it well beyond. They enjoy the hunt—the screams.

Bloodhounds have similar abilities, but they have the sense that can find a Burner. It's bad enough that they can know when a Burner is nearby, but they have an extra sense that goes well beyond. Oh, by the way, a Burner is me. I know, a strange name for someone who is cold and controls ice, but that's what I'm called. It's bad enough when a Bloodhound is near, but no one can ever use powers on them, which is a real kick in the butt, let me tell you. I am only able to use my powers like those ice blades, but if I tried to freeze a Bloodhound, he'd know more than just the preliminary stuff. He'd breathe my powers right in and be able to track me to the ends of the earth. The only one I have ever made the mistake of throwing my powers at tracked me until I killed him.

Even now his silent scream haunts my memories.

Which is why as I write this, the Fire Burner over there staring at me, I am so incensed that he was so stupid. He threw his fire at *the guy! Just like that! Idiot! The Bloodhound has his scent. If the Fire Burner's with me, then the Bloodhound will find me too. I should get back to what I was doing—where I was going.*

But can I abandon a fellow Burner...again?

CHAPTER 5

"Get down!" the new arrival yelled. I was having trouble taking in this new piece of information. I don't know where he came from. He was just there on the edge of the bank, reaching his hand out. But his look! I couldn't even breathe. Had the Breather been this flummoxed when he had seen me?

This person was more beautiful than anyone I had ever seen before. Hair like a golden mane flowing down to his shoulders. A clean, smooth face as if carved from the purest marble. Not a God, not a mortal—far beyond both. His lean muscles looked underfed but were still prominent under his black turtleneck and thick pants.

I couldn't even fathom why he had told me to duck. Couldn't understand why. Then I knew as a bullet was heard overhead that burst into melting flame.

"Hey," I said. My lips were slack, my jaw loose. I have never felt cold. But right there, I felt really warm, especially around my cheeks. "How are you?" Wow…Stupid question for one hundred!

But his eyes were wide, taking me in, forgetting the

Bloodhound just across from us. Of course, I was too. "What's your name?"

Wow, this whole conversation was stupid! Death was watching us, amused, probably wondering what he could do to our corpses, and we were dazed and confused by the mere sight of one another.

I suddenly was aware of the Breather aiming his gun for me again. I shook my head and pulled up an ice shield as another bullet shot through the night.

"Oh my god, what in hell is wrong with me?" I yelled. Had I lost all common sense?

"Good question for us both. But there's time for that later!" the guy yelled. "Gotta fry this guy!" Billows of flame burst from his pointed finger—traveling in a shining line right at the Bloodhound.

"No!" I screamed. I had no idea what was going on. My addled brain only gave me two facts. One, this guy was a Burner. Two, he had just thrown power at a Bloodhound. Digory just laughed and spread his hands wide. The flame met his body, but like I expected, it just suddenly started funneling right into Digory's nose. He gulped it in with deep breaths.

"Run!" I urged, but the new guy just stood there.

"He isn't burning. Why isn't he burning?"

His confusion was almost comical if he hadn't been breath-stealing gorgeous. Great. I had just met a Burner who had no clue about how our lives worked. That meant I would have to be the one to explain it to him.

After we escaped from the tracker who'd never stop.

Or I could leave the Burner on his own.

I don't know why, but I stayed with him. "Do you want to live or die?" I asked simply.

"Live, of course."

"Then listen to me!" I ran, not caring now if he followed.

But he did, and we left the Bloodhound behind. He didn't chase us. He knew he could get the Fire Burner anywhere. The Bloodhound breathed in the fire, pushing his face to the sky in pure ecstasy while he took on this Burner's essence, remembering him. Forever knowing his prey.

Together we ran. For the first time, I heard someone else's breath at my side. I wasn't alone. I wondered how long that'd last.

CHAPTER 6

Dear Diary,

Uh, hello, Diary? Umm, how do I start this thing every day? I woke up today at seven. Mommy and Daddy didn't wake me. I think becuz they are still fighting. But I should get ready for school. I like first grade. I like Miss Darlene. But mostly, I like not being here. I don't like the angry voices.

Daddy's knocking on my door. Better go see what he wants.

'm back again. I was wrong. There aren't any more angry voices. Mommy is crying. Daddy looks sad. But we're going to get ice cream! I like chocalte chip. But my favorite is pstashio. I want it in a cone.

I feel weird. Mommy is looking through my closet. She's grabbing my clothes. Okay, Diary, I'll tell you as it happens.

She has my little suitcase, the one Grandma gave me for the trip to California last year. Mom's putting my favorite red jeans in. My green shirt. All my other clothing I like. I didn't know ice cream was so far away we needed a suitcase.

She put my favorite plushie in too. I like sleeping with Fuzz Rumpus. Why do I need him?

One second.

~

I'm in the car now. Mommy wanted me to keep my notebook. She said, "Always write. Whenever you need someone to talk to, always write."

I'm a little concerned with her. She sure is getting sad when we're only getting ice cream!

But we're on our way. Daddy is in the front seat. He will not look at me. Mommy is spilling tears into her hand. And good grief are we driving far for ice cream!

We ran. Yes, *we*, after so long of being alone. But we ran the wrong way. We weren't going away from the nearby city. We were going back into it. And, no, don't expect me to know which city. I had been in so many in my life, they all kind of blurred together. All I knew was that I had found a place to settle down. And that was where I was taking Fire, back to my hideout. Back where I had run before. To the only home I've had since the facility.

I couldn't help throwing glances at him. Even with certain death on our tail, he was gorgeous. And every single time, I caught his eyes staring back. Peering. Probing. Desiring. Like I desired him.

But we had to run, not ogle. It didn't matter. His face was the flame, and I was the stupid moth. It was nice to know the other moth found my fire as attractive.

We weaved around streets. Always running. He followed me, trusting me instantly. Cool, yet terrifying. I didn't need anyone trusting me. Never again.

It was his look. That had to be it. The only reason I'd risk everything again instead of finally finding my own happiness. Here I was, heading back to my cage. I had found the sewer about a year ago. I had lived there. I had settled down, stopped running. That's where I was taking the guy so he could be safe from the Bloodhound. So he too could hide.

"How much further?" he asked.

My heart couldn't take the cadence of his voice. His smooth tones. Heartbreaking. Or heart-making. I'm not sure. This had never happened to me before.

"About a mile."

"Sheesh. Why are we running? Let's stop. I think I can try again."

I was glad, despite his words, that he wasn't stopping. He dogged my heels like he was born there. "Long story." My breath was smooth. I was used to this. "We have to get out of the—"

I heard a noise, foreign. It didn't belong in the city's cadence.

"Left!" I hissed and turned away from my hideout. The Bloodhound was nearby. I could practically feel his breath on my neck. He knew where the guy was. I pushed him into a door. It was a bathroom. Yes!

"Stay," I panted. I stared at the little hole in the wall we ended up in. I realized it was a bathroom of a gas station. All the pipes with running water should…

"Have to use the facilities?" the guy queried. I wished I knew his name!

I almost laughed. Yeah, like I'd risk going to the bathroom. "No. Water protects us. Just be quiet."

I closed my eyes and listened, using my honed senses. Footsteps. Quiet. Tentative. He knew we were close. Digory was trying to figure out why we had just dropped off his radar. I heard him slow outside, but then he broke into a run.

Arrogance! He thought there was no way he'd lose us, so he was backtracking to figure out where he'd lost our trail.

My eyes flashed open. I looked at the guy next to me and then shuddered. He was too beautiful. And he was staring at me.

"Come on. He won't be stymied for long."

"What's going on?"

I sighed. "He's tracking you. I have a place where he can't. I've lived there for about a year. I was lucky. I was running before."

"Running? From what? From that guy?"

I didn't want to answer. "From ones like him. You and me, we're not exactly like everyone else, or didn't you notice?"

The guy looked away. I could catch my breath without his eyes squeezing the air out of my lungs. "Where do you come from?" A nice way of saying, *where have you been all my life?* I wanted to know that too. He wasn't in the facility with me. I would have remembered.

"I ran from New York. Went south to Virginia. Headed toward New Mexico. Stayed in California. I was headed toward Washington until I met you. That's changed. Don't know any of the cities I've been in. I'm not good with that."

"You don't know the names of the cities you lived in?"

I was looking out the door now. I saw Digory's back, far off, leaving, but we had to wait just a bit longer.

"I don't know geography. It took me forever to realize there was a difference between county and country."

He laughed like I was joking. I didn't join in. "Well, welcome to San Francisco. And you're in California, or didn't you know that either?"

I kinda did. But I kinda didn't. "And that's where?"

"You really don't know much. Didn't you learn anything in school?"

I looked away. "Where I was going, I didn't need school.

Okay. Let's move. Fast, quiet. And no more questions. Believe me, your life is on the line."

He nodded. I only watched from the corner of my eyes. His beauty was destroying me enough without a full-on shot.

We ran again.

CHAPTER 8

The absolute beauty that Burners have makes no sense to me. I don't exactly look in the mirror much, but now that I've met another Burner, I get it. He's fantastic! All the planes of his face are perfectly aligned. I can look at him up close or from a distance, and he looks good from any angle.

Oops, I'm getting distracted. I have never felt this way in my whole life!

Okay, as far as I can tell, we're like the natural beauty of ice and fire. The winter makes such beautiful, intricate patterns when there's frost on the window or the leaves outside. A fresh blanket of snow never fails to elicit some kind of emotional response. How many poets and writers talk on and on about a winter's day?

And then there's fire. It's hot, dangerous, but how many people just stare at a burning building or a forest fire in absolute awe? How many hypnotists have used the flickering flame to entrance their audience?

Fire and ice both have the same awe attached to them. The power and thrill giving the looker a feeling of something just a bit beyond what is normally experienced in life.

So that's our beauty. As children, we are adorable. Then, as we hit puberty, we become breathtaking. Amazing. Unable to ignore.

I am using Fire as my expertise on this, though, because I can't take my eyes off him. Even as he paces in front of me and I try my best to think of all the facts I know about beauty, my heart is marching with his walk.

And his body has taken control of my eyes.

Yeesh.

Beauty is dangerous.

CHAPTER 9

"$\mathcal{H}$ere? You want us to stay here?" The sneer in his voice was clear. Where we were was a dismal opening to a sewer. It was a place I had claimed long ago when I was being hunted. I certainly didn't like seeing it again, no matter how beautiful I once thought it to be. I pushed my notebook into my backpack, which was starting to look a little gray instead of the vivid blue it once was.

I cursed inwardly. I didn't much like the place I had brought him to any more than he did. It was once my home, but I had run away from it. That train was supposed to get me out of this city. Why it had taken me so long, even I couldn't explain. I guess it's because as much as you can't go home again, you can't leave it either. But I certainly was willing to try after a year of imprisonment.

I glanced around, trying to see what this guy saw, and I had to admit, it wasn't pretty. This access hadn't been used in a while, and the shelf we sat on led to a ladder that descended into the lower areas. I had done my best to disguise this place that just connected to where all the sewage went. A few million miniature tiles covered the low ceiling above us. If you just climbed down the ladder, you'd see the sludge rivers stretching out for miles under the city through ugly gray tunnels. It was precisely why I had appreciated this hideaway so much. I knew that I couldn't be tracked here, and it was somewhat pretty—the closest I'd get to paradise.

Of course, with this guy here, suddenly it seemed a lot closer to paradise. He was just so beautiful. I wondered if that was why the Bloodhound who chased us had been so distracted. I certainly was. Still, I had caught my own beauty in every reflection I passed. I should have been immune to his beauty.

"Name!" I blurted out. Great, that was my version of "So, what do they call you?" I had planned to say it in my most casual voice and sound in control, not letting him know my hands were shaking more so than on the train. I tried to recover. "I mean, I'd like to know your name." *Yes! Much better.*

He gave me a grin and shrugged. "Rlah!"

"Excuse me?"

He cringed. "Sorry. It's Redmond. I can't seem to control my voice." His eyes traveled across my face. "How can you be so damned beautiful?"

I smiled for real. "It's a Burner trait. Didn't you know that?"

"What's a Burner?"

I sighed. *Here we go...*I could barely explain this to myself, let alone to a complete stranger who made me beyond nervous. "Burners are what we were born as. You are an obvious Burner, as you control fire. But ice burns too, and that's what I am."

"Ice burns?"

"Have you ever had a burn?" I remembered his control of fire. "Never mind. Dumb question. Well, if you had, you'd know that the worst thing you can put on it is ice because it burns the same. It can damage the tissue just as bad as the burn, got it?"

Redmond gave me a look. "Yeah, sure, makes complete sense. You've explained it so utterly well." He stalked the small area.

"Look, let me try again. Just sit down. This is your new home, so get comfortable. A Burner is a person who can control fire or ice. I found out when I was six that my skin freezes stuff. It has gotten more powerful as I've gotten older."

Redmond was trying. I could see that. He sat down on my makeshift couch. I had made this abandoned access point look as homey as I could. There was a cot with a pink sleeping bag...Stolen out of a laundromat—I'm not proud. A little set of folding chairs I put cushions on for a couch. A little sink where I washed dishes. A tiny cabinet right next to that with peeling paint. Most items were scavenged. Some were stolen. All had been left behind when I left. Now I was back in my same hole.

"Six?" Redmond asked. I liked his surprised look. It made his eyes wide so I could see every bit of his wonderful shaded gray irises. "Holy crap. I only found out recently..."

"Well, maybe it's different with a Fire Burner." Suddenly, curiosity overtook me. I already knew my story and what I found out about my own secret world. I was none too eager to relate it. But I still wonder how others like me lived. Ones on the outside. I had thought them all to be taken by the Breathers. "How'd you find out?"

Redmond gritted his teeth. "Car accident. Apparently, I exploded when my father hit another car after he'd been drinking. It saved me...but killed him and the family he hit. I knew immediately. So, I escaped."

"Escaped? Why?"

"Maybe it's different with ice, maybe you can control it perfectly. But I can't."

"No, it's not really different," I replied, remembering frozen water everywhere I touched.

"I've been on the streets for a while now. I didn't really want to go home. There was no one there, and I was afraid…" He was silent as he put his hands behind his head and leaned against the back of the faux couch.

"Afraid of what?"

He was silent such a long time that I thought he was done with the conversation. But he finally looked at me. I had to cover a gasp at the power, the intensity of his gaze. He was really too amazing for words. The allure we shared reached inside me. Like a thief, he crept into my hidden heart and stole it away, never to return to the ravaged remains. I wondered if he felt the same.

He certainly faltered as he tried to get out through a dry mouth, "I was afraid I would be brought in for murder. It was all me, Laoni. Dad hit them, but I burned them all. I was afraid to even leave the cave I found. I even singed that place up real good. Dammit!" He stood up and paced again. "It all seems so ridiculous. I burn things up. Me! I never even believed in spontaneous combustion before all this. Now…"

I recognized panic when I saw it. I had seen it enough times in the mirror. I deftly rummaged in my backpack, missing my notebooks and hitting my stash of food that I could actually eat. I threw Redmond a bag of Cheetos. "Eat. Everything seems better on a full stomach."

He shot me a glance and gave me a smile. I swear my heart stopped for several seconds.

"I appreciate it. Hmm, Cheetos. I almost remember what these taste like."

At my questioning look, he added, "Everything burns now. I get nutrition, I guess, but not much else."

While he was munching, sending comforting, crunching sounds through the air, I asked, "This cave you had, why'd you leave it?"

Redmond grimaced. Little plumes of smoke spilled out of his mouth as he answered. "I got…Well, being alone does things to the mind. I spent all my time staring at the walls, reading, running out to steal food, only to return to that wretched cave. I started wondering if my powers were really that dangerous. Worse, I couldn't remember who I was, what I was running from. My thoughts grew darker. I suddenly couldn't take even one more second in that place. I started running. Then I realized how stupid I was. No one would take me in. Hell, before my powers, *I* wouldn't take me in. I felt…like I was in that game Hangman. You know, every second, he comes into view a little bit more. I used to play that with my cousin. I would guess a letter, and more and more of the stick figure would appear. But it wasn't life the little dude was being drawn into, it was death. Every second of life was death. A full picture meant the guy swung. I felt just like that. The more I felt, the more I seemed doomed. Then I heard a large splash of water as I walked past the bridge."

I heard something hidden in his tone. Something dark, dejected. Lost. "Walked past…Is that what you were doing, just walking near the bridge?"

Redmond looked away. "Laoni, bridges are really tall, you know."

It sounded like a duh statement, but I got it. I knew what he was saying…or not saying. I wanted to ask why he'd just give up, but I knew I had been doing the same. Giving up. Not wanting to live one more day trapped like an animal. Hope had flown away from both of us. Why did I seem to hear its wings again while talking to Redmond?

Redmond continued with his story. "Instead, I ran down

to the bank and saw you. Oh man, you were so beautiful! I didn't know what— I couldn't fathom what I was seeing. But then that—" He shuddered and I felt warm, wishing he would stop moving his body. It made my own want to move with him, a lot closer. I tried to focus. This was serious.

"That man seriously jumped out of the window and freaking crawled down the moving train, climbing down the bridge columns after jumping free. I started fearing for your safety. He seemed…bad. Evil. He wants you…for more than just…Well, whatever he wants you for in the first place."

"Energy." I heard the derision in my voice. It made Redmond smile. "Of all the things, it appears we are better than oil for energy. Nice, huh? If we're caught, the Breathers will…I don't know, sell us so they can have power for something. Maybe one day we'll both run through a car's engine."

"When they catch us." He sounded sure of himself. I guessed he got it.

"They won't. We're safe here." I didn't mention that I was ready to freeze this whole place over rather than live another minute inside it. I had to forget that. Redmond needed me. And I was starting to need him. He slapped his fist into his palm. The little place was filled with the sound of his pounding feet.

"Please, sit, Redmond. We need to figure out what happens next, but your pacing won't help." I sat down on the couch and patted the seat next to me. I was trying to make it easier on him, that was all. But he took it the wrong way.

He blew some air out between his lips. "I, um, am not sure it's wise for me to sit next to you. Fire and ice don't mix. I haven't been exactly good around people. Even before I knew the truth about me, I gave my girlfriend a sunburn." He broke off and gave a harsh laugh. "I knew it hadn't been that sunny that day, but Karen hadn't realized. I've only gotten worse. I'd probably burn the poor girl now. I don't want to burn you."

"I'd probably freeze you first," I retorted. "I've never even had a boyfriend. I...gave my mom an ice burn when she said goodbye and I hugged her too tight."

Redmond looked intrigued. Suddenly, I wanted him to sit by me so badly just to see if I did burn him.

"Redmond, I want to see what happens. Sit. Touch me."

"Laoni, I don't think that is a good idea. You never had a boyfriend. If we could touch, I'd probably want to hold on. I haven't had human companionship in years."

"I've never had it," I said simply. Suddenly, nothing else mattered. I just wanted to hold him if I could. Was this some sort of madness inspired by this night? How close to danger I had come? The near escape. His beauty. How very alike we both were. "Couldn't we just check? Just two Burners sharing a human touch?"

"You mean if we can?"

I nodded, and he matched as if in a daze. Then he scooted close to me, both of us holding our breaths. I remembered too well my mother's screech when I had clung to her, begging her not to leave me with the Bloodhound. I didn't want Redmond to make the same sound, and I certainly didn't want to be burned!

He was on his knees now. He hadn't sat down. I slipped down to the floor next to him, and he knelt closer to me. I turned to him so we were face to face and we touched, our jeans against each other, but no skin contact, not yet. He held out one finger, and I reached out the same. Slowly, as if we were trying to recreate that God and man painting, we touched.

For a few seconds, we just cringed, waiting for...I don't know. Me to melt or him to extinguish, I guess. But nothing happened. We both carefully opened our eyes to stare at each other. I don't know who busted out laughing first, me or him, but soon we were both rolling on the floor.

I don't know when my laughter became tears. I bawled, ice balls streaming down my face. I never cried normal tears. Redmond quickly rolled next to me and clutched me to his front, letting our cheeks touch. No freezing, no burning, and I hugged him back. I hadn't had this comfort, the pure joy of being held, since my parents had sold me to the Bloodhound.

"What's your story?" Redmond asked, soothing me by touch. Letting me feel his skin by touching his hand to my face and hair. "Why are you alone?"

CHAPTER 10

I *have to write. I need to write. It's the only thing they left me with. I don't understand. I'm so scared. The room is too tiny. The walls are bare, gray. Not like the gray of clouds. Gray like the grime that scootches up around the shower at home.*

Home...Great. If I keep crying, I'll ruin my paper. No, I will not cry. I have to be a grownup now. When a girl has a mommy and a daddy, that's when she is allowed to stay little. I need to be big now.

Mommy's yell still is in my head. I hurt her! I know I did. I just wanted her to stop. She said yes to that tall man.

Oh, I am shivery. He is scary. He gave me such a mean grin. Diary, I can still see it all. I'll tell you, okay? Don't freak out. We'll be OK.

Mommy and Daddy drove into a big, abandoned parking lot where they met the man that had come to our house. They wanted it secret. No one knew. Even me. "How old is it?" he asked Daddy when we got out of the car. About me! As if I was an item. When Daddy told him, the mean man said, "Oh, we've got a long time together then."

He took my arm and pulled me forward. I didn't like his

touch, Diary. He wasn't right. He was just wrong. I pulled out of his clutches—funny, he didn't turn icy—and ran back to Mommy. I saw a glimmer of hope when I looked at her face. She wasn't sure! "Mommy, I want to go home." I hadn't liked that huge parking lot where we had driven to, had felt so bad when I realized we weren't going for ice cream, and I had screamed so loudly when they gave that evil man my little blue suitcase and said, "Take her."

It was like when we had the dog that kept having accidents, except, this time, I was the dog.

"Please, Mommy," I begged again.

"You'll treat her right...You won't hurt her."

The man gave a smile of oil and vinegar. "Don't worry. She'll be raised as sweet as any child can be. You're doing the right thing. These abominations (I had to look up that word when I got here, Diary—I was very mad when I found out what it meant) slip into nature. But as children, they are innocent. When she reaches the age of sixteen, that's when she'll have to worry."

"You're saying at sixteen you'll hurt her?" Mom demanded. Hope built up in my heart. I hate myself for that hope now.

"Honey," Daddy said, but he wouldn't look at me. "We can't keep her. Think of this as a mercy. She won't have any kind of life with her...disease. At least this way, Farrell assures us she'll live normally."

"Until sixteen!" Mommy shrieked. I held her tightly. Suddenly, frost built up on her pant leg and she looked down in horror. All sympathy and love vanished. She shook me off. "Get away! Take her. Just get her away from me!"

"Mommy!" I cried, holding tighter. She screamed out in utter anguish.

"You monster!" Daddy yelled and ripped me away. Suddenly he was blue all over.

"Daddy! I'm sorry! I won't do it again! Please take me home."

Farrell chuckled and slowly slid up to me. My powers stopped.

"Such dramatics. You'd better call an ambulance, sir and madam, but I will be leaving. Come along, little Burner."

And he gripped my hand tightly. When I refused to move, he picked me up and heaved me over his shoulder just like Daddy did with the bags of dog food we used to get. "No!" I yelled, but it was useless. As I was pushed into the big black van Farrell owned, my stomach started heaving. I could hear Mother's screams, Father's yells. My parents weren't mine anymore.

Daddy was still yelling. "Why wait until sixteen? Kill the evil thing now. Now!"

Even now...Sorry had to stop. I can't seem to feel my heart. I can't believe any of this. I feel older, really old. Even now, I keep expecting to hear Mommy and Daddy's voice outside this room, saying it was all a mistake, coming to take me home.

But it's been three weeks. I haven't seen much besides this room. I am writing everything down so I'll remember my way out when I escape. And I will escape. The problem is I don't know where I'd go. I can't go back home. They don't want me.

I kept telling myself on the drive to this place that I couldn't exactly blame Mommy and Daddy. I hurt them. Okay, they hurt me way deeper. Inside, where wounds couldn't heal, but still. I knew once they got over that, they'd take me back.

At least I knew that until Farrell smirked at me on the way inside. "I know that look, sweetheart. You still think you will be saved."

"I will be!" I screamed, aiming a kick at his shins. He just laughed.

"No, you won't. In my business, I've encountered two types of folks," he said. I struggled as he pulled me toward the humongous building. I couldn't see past my tears. "The ones who make decisions based on fear, and the ones who make decisions based on greed. Your father was the second category, and your mom the first."

He pulled me through two glass doors that had reflective glass so I couldn't see inside. There were huge hallways like at a hotel, and a front desk welcomed people in. The doors only opened and closed with key cards. The floors were of hard linoleum, gray like all the walls.

"I personally love the greedy ones. Offer them a cool million for their only child and they fold like a deck of cards. The fearful ones try to fight longer. Your mom was against this from the moment we started the game. But you saw her. You unleashed your powers and she turned on you. How silly. It was only your fear that let them loose. She wouldn't have been killed. You're not powerful enough. Mortals are silly."

It was then, Diary, that it became obvious. Farrell wasn't human. Suddenly, I got scared. Daddy and Mommy had believed it okay for me to watch all the movies that they did. One really gave me nightmares. There was this guy who was against the government and these men in black suits had taken him away. I thought that was what was happening to me.

But then I remembered. He said I would no longer be unharmed when I was sixteen. What was going to happen to me? It wasn't as simple as being held prisoner. He wanted me for something.

So, here I am. Older mentally, but not physically. I have to wait. I have ten years to figure out how to escape. So far, Farrell hasn't gone back on his promise. I've been fed well. He let me have my suitcase and my notebooks. No electronics at all, but he's given me a lot of games. I like Hangman. I even have a whole new wardrobe. All of it is some kind of strange plastic material that covers me from toes to neck. I feel a bit confined, but I like the look of my fingers and toes, all of them gloved. It looks cool, like I have blue fingers and toes instead of fleshy.

More importantly, I can't freeze anything. It keeps me so locked up I can actually drink water. Thanks to my freezing powers, it's been hard to drink water. I suppose one day, without this suit, I'll *have to just eat ice for any liquids. I can't believe being locked up could have a good side.*

The deep sadness that reminds me that I am no longer wanted by anyone except my jailers makes me cry. I am so lonely. But Farrell promises I'll meet some others like me soon. He seems to care about me. I don't know why. He plans to hurt me one day. How could he care?

CHAPTER 11

Redmond didn't take long to judge my parents harshly. As soon as I finished telling him about my first night in that prison, he jumped up and spit, "I hope they got frostbite!"

I didn't know how to take his statement. I'd never been defended before. I decided I liked it. But to be over charitable, I said, "I understand why they were so scared of me."

He knelt back down again, eager to stay in touch. This new connection between us was not romance, though I'd be lying to say certain thoughts didn't race through my brain as his cheek caressed mine. I hadn't had any real touch since I had hurt my mother. Even with Farrell's kindness toward me, he abhorred me. He had thought me unnatural and had made no pretense about what would happen to me when I turned sixteen.

As Redmond kept moving his face against mine, eager as I was to feel, his lips caught mine as well. It was a brief touch, but I practically jumped out of my skin. It was too intimate for strangers, but we both wanted it. Instead, we both pulled away, without sound crying out at losing the touch.

But we knew it wasn't right. We could touch each other. Being so overcome by each other wasn't a reason to throw away common sense. We could break each other so easily, and we needed each other.

"So, how long did you stay in that place?" he asked wretchedly as he stayed away from me.

"Six years. I got out of there at twelve and never looked back."

He clenched his hands into fists and started pacing again. I swear he was going to burn a hole right through the ground if he kept doing it. "So, at six, you were taken away and taken to a strange place. You're a bit tight-lipped about that place, too."

"I…"

"It's okay. I don't need to hear what hurt you. You left at twelve, and you've been alone since?"

I nodded. "And you? You had a girlfriend. A life. You weren't alone."

He didn't answer. His eyes drifted away, lost somewhere else. "You can be surrounded by people and still be alone, Laoni. My dad…He wasn't there for me. He liked the bottle more than his son. And my friends? My girlfriend? They thought I was a downer. I've always been a pessimist. The glass isn't half-empty, it's gone."

I found a laugh hidden in my throat. Quite a miserable pair, weren't we?

"I had friends," I quickly noted. "So, I win!"

He turned on me with surprise, but then he saw my mischievous smirk. "Ha, that's nice. Humor. What a concept when right outside is a man who wants to rip our heads off and pour our juices into an engine."

I giggled and tossed a handful of ice at him. As I expected, it melted before it even touched him. He stared for a few seconds. "So, do you know how many there are? Of us? Of the Breathers?"

I shook my head. "I've only met a few other Burners." I wasn't in the mood to explain more, and I think he understood that. "As far as Breathers go, I'm not even sure where they come from. Their sole purpose in life is to catch us and put us away. There was this girl I knew once. She said that Breathers were bred." I shuddered. "I don't know how or why, but they were brought into life to chase us Burners. Burners are natural. Breathers aren't.

"That makes me feel better," Redmond said. "Because when I kill the freak, I won't feel guilty. What a change of pace that'll be."

I shook my head and started making my cot for Redmond. But he stopped me. He put one finger on my arm.

"Take the bed. I like the hard floor."

"A gentleman," I responded.

"I try. Though you can't take the evil out of the fire, you can at least burn nicer."

An odd statement. He was really down on himself, wasn't he? Redmond was the most interesting guy I had ever met. We were so completely different. Our powers proved that. Yet, he felt the same as I did.

But, I reminded myself, we aren't the same. *He risked his life for you. All you've ever done was run.*

CHAPTER 12

*D*ear Diary,

    I met more kids today, people like me. I have met a lot, actually. My first friend was a girl named Cindy. But since I've been here, more have been showing up. There were already a few kids here. Farrell is treating us all like we're just kids, like this is one gigantic school. We're expected to eat at the same time. The only thing we're not expected to do is study. No reason, Farrell says. I'm not sure if it's because of what he promised at sixteen or if he doesn't expect us ever to go out into the world.

    I don't like it either way. I take every chance to study. I like English, to be honest. And math's okay. I dislike science, so I don't study that as much as I should. The only reason I do at all is because one day I plan to be out in the world. I don't want to be a dolt when I get out of here. There are no teachers here, and there are very few kids who like studying. Only me and a boy named Bobby spend any kind of time in the library. We nod to each other when we end up in the library at the same time, sometimes sharing facts about what we're looking at. I've fallen in love with other languages.

    Anyway, the other kids are cool. None of us can hurt each other thanks to our wardrobe. Cindy, a younger girl, has latched on to me. I'm not sure which she is, Fire or Ice. Yeah, there are two kinds. Not that any of us have a chance to use our powers. These clothes are never removed. They stay on no matter what. I have latched on to Belinda, a Fire Burner. She's so cool with this long brown hair that swishes when she walks. She is much older, but she has been my friend since she arrived. We're all friends. We all need each other.

I know it's been a while since I've written, but to be honest, I only feel like writing in this unemotional and one-sided thing when I'm depressed. But I actually haven't been. Oh my gosh, I can't believe I wrote that! This place is a prison. I've been stolen from my family, my life, and here I am saying I've been happy!

Still, it's not bad. Belinda is totally my best friend! She's full of stories and songs. She's already spent most of her time rallying our spirits. She believes we'll all be okay. Her optimism makes me happy. The smile that breaks out on her face makes all of us laugh, even the pessimistic Erin. Oh, she's new. She's angry all the time. She was taken from her bed, or so she says.

They are the two constants in my life now. While Belinda is the sun, Erin is the dark cloud, constantly hovering around my bright spot. I'm in the middle, trying to remind myself which side I'm on. Cindy is oblivious. She likes Erin. I don't.

See, Erin believes we're all doomed. She doesn't hesitate to remind me that we've been brought to a prison. That we all have abilities. That we're all going to die. Belinda will be the first since she's fifteen.

I don't believe Erin. It isn't true! They were trying to scare me, Farrell and Mom and Dad. I agree with Belinda. She thinks we'll all be let go when we're old enough. A few older kids have already left us. "Graduated," according to Farrell, even though we don't ever study.

Every afternoon, we're allowed to run around a big, grassy yard. That's when Belinda and I sit down with Cindy, my shadow

41

(though she's not much my shadow anymore: Erin's taken the honor). Our little dark cloud Erin keeps up a countdown of how soon we'll lose Belinda. We all ignore her and lie under the brilliant sky and try to come up with answers.

We can't just be being brought up for destruction! It makes no sense. Belinda and I have the best answer. We're all mutants. We have to learn our powers. Once we do, we'll be utilized in secret government programs where we'll save the world!

We needed code names, of course. I am Strawberry Ribbon thanks to the ribbon in my hair. I wish I had worn a different hair ornament, but I guess Strawberry Ribbon is better than Banana Barrette!

Belinda gets to come up with the names because she's the oldest, or so she says. She gave Erin the name of Little Ladybug. I'm glad that's not my name. Strawberry Ribbon isn't great, but I hate bugs.

Erin, of course, had to ruin our game today— Oh crap. I said game. It's not a game! It's not. I know it's not. Stupid Erin! She says it's a game, and she's got me believing it! Today Erin said that she hoped our "game" (quotation marks emphatically entered here to show my rebellion at the idea; so there, Erin) could keep us happy when our captors are skinning us alive.

Ugh! As I write this, I hate her. Why is she like this? Belinda and I told Erin all the facts. When facts don't add up, the answer those facts point to has to be wrong. I told Erin that this facility costs money. Money to feed us, to house us, to give us games, clothing. Why would they do all this just to execute us? Answer bell! They wouldn't! We are being protected. Farrell, I think, even likes us all. He always smiles at us.

Stupid Erin! Sorry, Diary, but her words haunt me this evening like one of those tunes rolling around. Oh, I have to write them down even though I...Great, I feel so stupid. If I write it down, it'll make it true or something.

It won't! It won't. Right? Right. So, I'm going to write it down so it'll get the hell out of my head.

Erin said, "Farrell treats us like animals. Like cows reared for slaughter."

Erin is just...mean, that's what she is.

Farrell likes us. He feels like our father.

That's it. Words, get out of my head!

~

*D*iary, this day is awful. Belinda dead. Can't even... Can't believe. Tomorrow. No way today. God, she's dead!

CHAPTER 13

edmond was a horrible houseguest! He was as horrible a guest as this sewer entrance was a house. He didn't like being cooped up. He resented my solo trips outside. He wanted to go out even though I told him how dangerous that was and he didn't like being alone.

My heart felt shriveled from disuse, but it beat painfully every single time I returned and saw his eyes light up at my return.

My vanity was being coddled, stoked, and it was starting to roar. Redmond was a terrible houseguest but a wonderful friend. It turned out we had a lot more in common than just being Burners.

We both loved to run—good thing given our normal habit of being chased. We had the same taste in songs. We laughed together when I brought back a music player filled to the brim with rap songs and then yelled "shut it off!" at the same time. We both hated rap but loved the classic tunes. Music surely tamed these savage beasts.

We both woke up early. We were morning birds, not night owls. We even enjoyed pizza the same way: pineapple, mushrooms, and pepperoni. We hated television shows but adored movies. We also loved to read. I was quick to point out *Jane Eyre* as my favorite classic, and what surprised me was that he liked it as well but adored *Moby Dick*.

"Whales getting killed?" I asked, my back pressed against the tiled wall while my legs lolled over the edge and swung back and forth. I wanted to lean against Redmond's chest, but we had silently agreed after that kiss to stay away from each other. Physically dangerous we may not be, but we sure were mentally.

So, we were playing it totally casual. We didn't need to touch each other. We were just friends.

Redmond laughed as he chewed the corner of his pizza, smearing the sauce on his cheek and looking incredibly amazing. "*Moby Dick* is not about killing whales. It's adventure. It tells the tale of how whaling ships operated. Ishmael lived in a wonderful time where he could just take to the seas!"

"And die a horrible death," I joked.

"A pretty tragic fate hit Rochester at the end of *Jane Eyre*, didn't it? At least Ishmael was unharmed."

"But there's no romance!"

"Nothing is more romantic than Queequeeg and Ishmael!"

I groaned. What a statement! "No, no, no."

"Okay, okay. I can't convert you it seems."

"No, I'll read it and even try to get past that part where Ishmael is peeling the whales like oranges this time. Oh and that long chapter on the color white."

Redmond stared at me. "So, you have read it?"

"Once or twice. I had a hard time getting through it."

Redmond laughed and put his crust on his paper plate.

"Eat the crust, Redmond. You shouldn't waste it."

"Okay, Mom…"

"Ouch!" I retorted. I didn't like being called that. There was nothing motherly about my feelings for Redmond. We are friends, I reminded myself.

He spread his hands as if to say sorry. His eyes shot to my face and then back down again, lingering on certain parts but trying to remain a gentleman. "Laoni...I want to do something."

My heart jumped. Oh, something sounded good! But did I want to? *Friends*, I spit inwardly and readied myself for the negative response.

"I want to go out."

Oh...I didn't expect that. Well, good. Better...wait, what? "No way."

"But this is a waste of time. We have no proof that the Bloodhound caught my scent."

"Yes, we do. I know what it looks like." I gestured for him to pick up his plate and toss it to me to put in the trash.

"We can't stay here forever!" His eyes followed me.

"We don't have to. Just give it time and we'll figure out a way of killing that Bloodhound. We have to give him time to get so frustrated he'll forget to think. Then we'll draw him into a trap."

"We...are going to kill him?"

"It's the only way." I flexed my hands and turned to stare at the darkened tunnels that protected us. "Otherwise, he'll never stop coming after you."

Redmond sat back hard against the wall. "Then what? What kind of life do people like us have?"

My mind flashed back to Belinda's face the last time I saw her. "There is a place where Burners live in peace. A better place. The island is huge and can't be burned. No one can follow unless they are Burners."

Redmond wrinkled his brow. "Sounds like a fairy tale."

"It was a fairy tale," I admitted. "Someone long ago told it to me. Truth is, I didn't believe in it for a very long time. I get so sick of running though. It's gotta exist. I have to believe that now or else . . . We just have to figure out where it is. I was heading there when the Bloodhound found me."

"Heading where?" Redmond exploded, jumping up to pace again. He rarely stopped for long. "A mythical land where we're safe? Going to find Narnia next? Or maybe Professor X's School for the Gifted?"

"Redmond, it exists!" I said. "I know it."

"How? Do you have any proof?"

I shook my head.

"Then how do you know?"

"I have faith. I can't believe in anything else."

Redmond was silent.

"Go ahead, say what you want. I can take it." I pulled up the bag and crunched the plates inside. Even in this place of waste, I wouldn't trash it.

"I..."

"Redmond, we're Burners. We're united, you and me. We could be the only ones left of our kinds." I carefully ignored my screaming guilt. "Let's say what we think. If I can't handle your opinion, I shouldn't exist when there are far worse forces in this world I have to endure."

"Alright, but you asked for it!" he retorted.

"I believe I did, yes. Get on with it."

"I think it's incredibly naïve to believe such a place exists!" He stood up and pushed his fists into his hips like he was getting ready for a fight. "And based on what? No logic. No facts. Just faith!"

"And isn't it also naïve to believe in a girl who can freeze water? A boy who can turn the very air around into burning flames? A man who can get engulfed in fire but survive *after* climbing down a train and a bridge. Our lives are a fairy tale!"

Redmond couldn't argue with that. *Ha! Got him!*

But I'd be patient. I resisted the urge to go nah, nah, nah. "You see? I believe it's incredibly naïve to believe it can't possibly exist just because you haven't seen it."

Redmond started to grin. "Okay, you've got me. I guess I'm still being a pessimist. But just look at it my way. I had nowhere to go before I found you. But even after we get out of our prison here, I'll have nowhere to go."

I closed my eyes. "Hey, nowhere is better than where we are now. Or do you like being trapped? Forced to live in a hole that is meant for waste?"

Redmond sighed loudly to let me know what he thought of this whole idea, I'm sure.

"Okay, you've got a point! Let's go chase a unicorn together."

"Alright!" I said, and we clapped our hands in a high five. We let go extremely quickly. This touch thing was still out of bounds. I never wanted to let go. But I wouldn't depend on him—and he couldn't depend on me.

CHAPTER 14

*O*kay *Diary, I have to write again. I have to tell Belinda's story. Well, what little I know of it. She has to be remembered. It started...I guess six months ago. Belinda turned sixteen, but she was left alone.*

I remember now laughing and teasing Erin as the minutes ticked closer and closer to Belinda's birthday, 6:02 pm. It hit and we cheered. We were given a cake, and Belinda blew out the candles.

"See, Erin," I'd said, "is she dead? Did the guys come and take her away?"

Erin couldn't answer. She knew she was wrong. We had all—even despite my beliefs—thought they'd storm our common room, get Belinda, and drag her off kicking and screaming the moment she turned sixteen.

Great relief filled our area. We celebrated with games and talking. We all were excited to see that Farrell had been lying about something bad happening when we turned sixteen. What a joke!

I laughed so hard.

A week passed and we were happy.

Then...

I wish whatever it was out there in the universe that granted birthday wishes that I had just stayed in bed when Farrell took Belinda.

He did it secretly in the night. I had to go to the bathroom. I saw him inject a needle into her neck. She didn't struggle—she couldn't. Then he put her on a stretcher and wheeled her away.

"She's sick," I'd murmured to myself. And it could have been a great explanation. She had been able to get past our protective clothing. She had started fires for our amusement. So, maybe they just had to help her out.

That's why I didn't follow. I did nothing as he left the room. I just went back to bed. The next morning, we were allowed out, but there was no sign of Belinda. And I felt so cold, something I'd never felt before. Not on the outside, but inside. There seemed to be a rope of solid ice wrapped around my insides. I listlessly walked around the yard.

Something caught my eye across the way. A door that was always tightly shut and locked was...open. Just a slight gap. No one else saw it. I always have had an eye for detail, Diary. I almost wish I didn't after what I saw next. Still, that detail helped in my escape.

Even if it did lead to horror before I did.

No one ever watched us. The facility was too locked up—typically. How had the door been left unlocked? I went toward it, not knowing exactly why.

But my eyes weren't deceiving me. It was open. How? The only clue was a melted lock. From...fire. Weird.

I probably should have stayed put. Farrell would not be happy if I investigated. But...I did.

I pushed that door open to a long corridor. Facts started clicking in my mind. Belinda...She had somehow melted this lock. But why? How? Could her body have burned off that stuff Farrell had put in her? Even if she had, why would she struggle?

And she had struggled. I saw singed marks along the walls. No...Belinda, why did you struggle? Did I even want to know?

I followed the marks. I wish I hadn't.

No, I don't. Belinda had left the trail for me to follow. So, I did.

It's why I had to run. Why we all would have to get out of there. Everyone was off at lunch while we were at play.

They hadn't bothered to cover Belinda's body.

She was in a morgue. There were a lot of those tables that pulled out of the walls.

Belinda was going to be put in there.

She was dead. She hadn't "graduated." She had been murdered.

She couldn't even flicker anymore. Her whole body seemed thinner, her skin shadowed and gaunt. Her face was pasty and lean as if...

My mind couldn't figure out the "as if..." part. I didn't know what happened to her. I still don't.

All I knew was I had to escape. Erin was right. I wanted to tell her that. But something else happened.

No, I can't tell you tonight, Diary. I'm free, but I'm being chased.

Farrell is hunting me.

The morning and the evening were the same in the sewers. Everything was the same. Yet, when I woke up on the day we wanted to head out to look for the mythical place that Belinda told me about, everything felt different.

Could there be hope burning inside me? Maybe it was Redmond and having someone else to run with. I didn't know. But I was a regular, gosh-darned optimist as I woke up and started stretching.

While I finished packing all of my worldly goods back into my backpack and tied my sleeping bag up to carry under my arm, my heart felt a lot lighter than it had in years. Maybe it was because I was finally getting a chance to do what I should have done when I escaped—help someone run instead of only looking out for myself.

I glanced at Redmond. He was lucky I had an extra sleeping bag that I had gotten *just in case*. I had gotten a lot of things over the years just in case. So, he was sleeping in that brown bag—and now he was waking up himself. I fought back a silly grin. His beauty was driving me wild, and I only now knew how hard it had been for that bloodhound when he pulled my hood off. For years, I had been disgusted with everyone I met. The ones who stared after me. The men who crashed cars. The women who stopped me in the store just to chat. I thought they were pathetic. But now…If Redmond passed me on the street, I'd be just as pathetic.

"What's up?" he asked. One eyebrow, and only one, rose while the other stayed in place. I never knew that that one little facial idiosyncrasy was my dream trait in a guy, but now it was.

"What do you mean?" I asked and quickly busied myself with making sure I had picked up all my stuff. I knew I had, but I didn't want to admit that I was just staring at Redmond.

"You were staring at me." He wouldn't let it go so easily. Great. He was as stubborn as I was.

"It's what they all do. Haven't you noticed?" I once more checked the area where I was sleeping and the makeshift kitchen. This time I did it to make sure I really left nothing behind. I had lost so much over the years. The precious mementos I had were hard won. The sad thing was that until Redmond, they were my only companions.

"Noticed what?" Redmond was just as anxious to get going as before, but he was curious about what I was going to say. I realized that I'd never told him how alluring we were to others. I had kept it hidden even with all my explanations that we shouldn't be together because it was all fake. He had no idea how truly beautiful he was.

I stopped and looked at him with a slight sneer on my face. "It started when I was fourteen. It happened for…" I looked away. I had almost told him how it happened for Belinda at the facility, but I couldn't tell him about all the ones who I left behind. "It is tied up with our abilities. We're beautiful. What?" I didn't like his look. It told me to confide in him. I just didn't want him to stop looking at *me*. "Didn't you get stared at? You're the most handsome guy on Earth. You could walk into a modeling agency and get a job."

Redmond frowned. "No. I wasn't aware of that. I mean, I guess it makes sense. Everyone I knew wanted to take me down a peg. I never knew why. Maybe it was because they thought I was too good looking. I told you I was alone."

"Oh." I wanted to take his hand, but I knew that Burners were too appealing for their own good. We didn't need to be distracted like last time. "Well, it comes with our abilities, I guess. You ever look at ice or fire? I mean, really look?"

He hoisted his own backpack up on his shoulder and made a gesture with his head. I was to talk while we walked. This place was making him crazy. It certainly wasn't good for my peace of mind either. When I first found this place, that Farrell guy was right around the corner. It was only a block from here where I made my first kill.

"Fire is so beautiful you want to touch it. Even though it's a destructive force, when it leaps up into the night sky... you're in awe." I started climbing the ladder that opened to the street. My heart beat in that familiar fear, but this time it was for Redmond. His scent was firmly in that bloodhound's nose. When would we have to fight? "And ice, it destroys if it comes too early. Frost can decimate a field of crops, but its patterns make your breath fall away."

Redmond nodded. "Is that why I can't stop staring at you?" I could feel his warmth on my heels as I moved the manhole above me to slip out onto the street. It was a nice crisp morning—my kind of morning. The stars were still out, and the dawn sky was slowly obliterating them.

"Exactly. We both are taken by beauty. But we're not alone. It has saved my life. It saved my life right before I jumped off the train. The ones chasing us, they are taken in for a brief time before recovering. I usually flee before they recover."

Redmond chuckled and looked around. I wondered what he was looking for until he pointed to a little red Mazda parked on the street. "There's our ride."

I laughed but then realized he was serious. "Redmond, you can't steal a car."

"Yes, I can. And there's no time to convince you." He jogged over to the car. He fiddled with the door for a moment, and I saw a plume of smoke coming up from the handle. I had no choice but to follow him. I had never stolen a car before. Probably because I don't know how to drive. This life I led didn't allow morals. Still, it did seem wrong to steal someone else's car. I couldn't help but think of the poor person who would leave for work or something and find an empty space. It had to feel pretty bad, especially if that job was the difference between living on the street like I was or staying in a house.

I told myself to get over it. With what I had done to stay alive, I had no room to talk when it came to illegal activities. Plenty of people had suffered because of me.

I didn't say a word until Redmond unlocked the passenger side door and I got in. "So, tell me how you're going to do this." I needed to know so I could forget the person who owned the car. I could already see signs of who it was. A little plastic pacifier hung from the mirror, maybe from a baby, and there were pieces of paper spread out under the window with squiggles of "Great job!" and "A+" on them, while a few dollar bills were in a little tray in the center. I pocketed that without morals. I called myself a hypocrite as Redmond explained.

"So, get ready to be amazed, Snow," he said. I only shot him a look at the sudden nickname. But I was happy for it. It kept us in a friend zone. It protected us. "Engines work with something called internal combustion. Small explosions make the engine go. Now normally a key starts the process, but with this..." He wiggled his fingers. A little dancing flame appeared and shimmered in the early morning air. "I can create my own explosions."

"Oh, so you can also send your power further away from you. I figured you could only use your body as a conduit."

Redmond closed his eyes. I could practically see the effort on his face. Then the engine roared to life. "Yeah, despite the inconvenience, my powers are useful. Now, I'd prefer a Ferrari or a Mustang, maybe a Jeep, but this car is adequate."

I giggled as he pulled away from the curb and shot across the morning brightened street. "Seriously? You want a fast car? Isn't your life fast enough?"

Redmond shot me a glance. "The faster you are, the more your past won't catch up."

"You act as if you need justice," I noted. It was nice to move this fast. I was so used to walking or running. "You didn't kill those people. Your father did."

Redmond made a disgusted sound deep in his throat. He wouldn't listen to me. Funny, he trusted me with his life, but with his past, I wasn't allowed in. "Yeah, and we're in a car again, in case you couldn't tell. One wrong move and poof! One more murder."

I shook my head. "You're being an idiot. I wouldn't burn. Remember?"

"Let's just run. Let's not talk. Not now. Not in the car."

I sobered up. It was nice to ride in a car and not among other people for a change, but I couldn't forget we were being chased.

"So, where is the mythical land?" he asked.

"Head toward the highway, toward Washington."

Redmond's eyes stayed on the road, but I could see his

desire to roll them. "Just toward Washington? That's where we're going? No city name? Not Seattle or…Well, I can't name any other cities in Washington."

"It is a legend, silly. And it could be worse. We don't need to follow any stars or anything." I looked out the window. "We'll know it by the shape of the mountain near it. It looks like a woman's face."

"Like, a woman lying on her back or a profile?"

"I don't know. All I have are little clues." My head fell against the rest. "Find the lady of the mountain, then the boat to freedom will be caught. It will take us to the Island of Difference."

Redmond groaned so loud it filled the car. I wish I could say it annoyed me, but it just made me feel warm. I guess everything about Redmond made me feel warm.

"A lady of the mountain? That's insane. I've never heard of a mountain like that. Traveling there means going over lots and lots of dry land. There won't be any islands." I watched as his fingers tapped the steering wheel in succession.

"The path will be revealed if we head to Washington. That's what I was told."

Redmond said nothing more. I quickly took his hand and rubbed his knuckles. "Redmond, I know it's out there. And you know that anything worth having is worth fighting for. The more we struggle, the more we'll find peace—a place."

"I just don't understand," he admitted. We reached the highway and he drove faster. "How can you trust in a place where the only direction you have is Washington and a freedom boat near a strange mountain that leads to an island where Burners are safe?"

I didn't answer. I couldn't explain. Instead, I pulled his hand up and kissed the same knuckle I had rubbed. He didn't ask any more questions. He melted into my touch until I dropped his hand. Then he didn't remember our conversation. I shouldn't have used that dirty tactic, but I didn't know how to respond. Everything in me was based on faith. Faith that Belinda was telling the truth. And it was faith that said she was somehow still with me, guiding us. And that if we reached that island, we would be happy.

It took only an hour of driving for our Bloodhound to catch up. I was drifting off when Redmond cursed.

"He's behind us."

CHAPTER 16

*D*ear Diary,

Belinda is kind of scaring me. She has been in her room for days without coming out. Farrell says it's because she's a moody teenager, but I don't know why that should mean anything to a friend. It's been four days since her birthday, but she doesn't seem as happy as she was that day. I go and see her every day, but she says nothing. She does nothing. She was recently tested for... Well, I don't know what. Maybe she's sick. That would explain why she's in her room.

But today made me even more nervous. Belinda seems angry. I went to her room and she pulled me inside, looking up and down the hallway outside her door. When she didn't see anybody, she turned to me and said, "Laoni, you're my best friend."

That information thrilled me to my toes. I had never been anyone's best friend before. And to be a friend to someone four years older than I am, it's incredible. I feel important. I know we've known each other for like four years now, but she has never said anything like that before. The rest of her statement scared me more than thrilled me, though.

"I don't want you staying here. I don't want you dying here."

At first, I thought she was joking, but she was so serious. Oh, Diary, I think she thinks she's going to die! Damn that Erin! She must have spread her paranoia. When she didn't get her way when Belinda turned sixteen, she must have tortured Belinda with her own worries. I tried to tell her Erin was being stupid. But Belinda shook her head.

"No, Erin is the person who sees truth the best. I don't have much time. Farrell is no longer looking at me."

I wondered what that meant. All the people here looked at us. When we're young, we're like dolls. They couldn't stop saying, "Aren't they precious?" and "How very beautiful the Burners are." It always made me feel special. I know it kind of makes Belinda feel weird now that she's sixteen. She's getting stranger looks. I think one of the janitors is already in love with her. It's strange for a forty-five-year-old man to look at a sixteen-year-old like he wants to date her, but he doesn't creep me out or anything.

Not that he can do anything about his desires. We are kept away from everyone but Farrell and what he calls the Breathers. Still, I know they all look at us the same way. When young, we're beautiful dolls to be coddled; and when we get older, we're objects of desire. To have Belinda worry because Farrell isn't looking at her seems weird.

I said as much to Belinda. Oh, Diary, her words make me shiver even now.

"He's keeping himself safe from my beauty. He knows he has to become immune to it. If he desires me in any way, shape, or form, he won't be able to murder me."

I slapped Belinda at that. I feel sooooooooooo ashamed now. I slapped my best friend! She looked at me like I was being stupid. Like Erin would look at me. I AM NOT BEING STUPID!!!!!!!

Belinda is paranoid. Even though I slapped her, she still pulled me to her chair and held my hands so I couldn't move. "You can get free. It's too late for me. I have too many people watching me, but there are kinks in the system. If you're ready when I...I go, you can guide all the others out. Erin will help you. Then you'll be free."

"Where would I go? My parents don't want me."

Belinda is so insane. She told me a fairy tale. According to her, there's an island of people like us. We have to travel to Washington to a mountain lady and find a boat called Freedom. Then it will take us to an island where we can live happily ever after. I would be able to see the outside of this place again. I've always wanted to see forests...the ocean. We are prisoners here.

But, no! I was being stupid. Belinda and Erin are stupid. So what that none of us are older than sixteen and Farrell had hinted that we'd be hurt at sixteen? He also said we would graduate. Which meant we would leave here and go out to the normal world. Have normal lives.

I won't believe otherwise. I don't think a stupid island exists where we'd be free. We're happy here, even if we are controlled. We will graduate, I know we will, even though I feel stranger and stranger every day. We're all like ticking time bombs. My own special suit had to be upped just yesterday. Now I feel like I'm wearing sweaters all the time. It's lucky that I don't feel heat any worse than I feel cold.

There is no island.

There are no worries.

Farrell loves all of us.

Belinda and Erin are stupid. That's it. End of day, end of Diary. Maybe tomorrow I can spend time with someone else here. I'm tired of worrying.

I don't want Belinda or Erin to be right.

CHAPTER 17

Redmond had, of course, assumed that Digory was with us based on his knowledge of movies. There was a big black car driving behind us. What sucked was that he turned out to be right. It drove up behind us quickly and smashed right into our back end. Once again, I felt a small bit of guilt flare up. The owner of this car would never get it back now.

Of course, staying alive was much more important!

"Keep driving!" I yelled as we fishtailed across the road and Redmond tried his best to avoid other cars.

"Maybe we should stop and fight!" Redmond said, but I noticed his foot shoving the gas pedal against the floor.

"It doesn't work on them. Nothing works on them. Only physics, like if their car hit a six-foot tall ice wall!"

I reached my hand back over the seat and concentrated harder than I ever had before in my life. I could ice things, but I had never tried to create a wall out of nothing.

Could I do it?

The funny thing is that in dangerous situations, you can do things you never thought you could. At my behest, a wall shot up in front of the Bloodhound's car and he smashed right into it.

"Yes!" I yelled. Redmond didn't stop, but I kept looking back. The Bloodhound was thrown through the window. Murderers didn't believe in seatbelts, I guess. But even though he was thrown about a hundred feet, he stood up again. I could tell he didn't look good from here, but he wasn't dead. Which meant he could still follow Redmond. In my mind, I still saw Redmond's fireball engulf him while he stood there, breathing it in, getting Redmond's scent forever. My Redmond, now a scent in a Bloodhound's nose.

"Is he gone?" Redmond asked. "That seemed way too easy."

"No," I muttered as the figure walked toward the road. "Just drive as fast as you can. Toward Washington."

CHAPTER 18

*D*iary,

It's been years since I've written. There just wasn't any time. Quite a few times I thought I was safe, but I'm not. I won't ever be. I'm scared. I had to write just to keep my sanity. I'm so scared I'm shaking. I know he's after me.

I found my way out of the woods behind the facility. I got out. I was free. At least that's what it felt like. But I think he saw me leaving. He knew. He's following me. But for the first year, he let me run. Let me get used to it. I thought he had let me go.

Farrell knew I'd seen something. I had changed, and he was very observant. He'd been watching me more than anyone else. Why did he kill Belinda? What is it what we do when we turn sixteen that terrifies them so much? Or maybe it doesn't terrify them. Farrell gets more eager as he sees us grow. Like he will get something from it. Something good. There's no fear. It's something more. Belinda was killed because of it. Will I be killed?

No! No! I swear it. I've gotta live for Belinda and...for the others I left behind. I betrayed her. I betrayed them all. It just seemed too hard to get them and run. I just ran when I saw the open door. I knew I had to save myself. Why do I feel so icky inside?

I needed to lose those clothes first. I was fine inside them, but I wanted to have power. I shredded the things that kept me contained. I felt so...I don't know how to describe it. Free, but not really. I felt like I was me again after all those years of wearing it, not even removing it to bathe. It's a long story, Diary.

I lived and breathed in that suit. It's long gone now. I had lots of time to practice. I wonder if that's what Farrell wanted me to do. Practice. Maybe he's, like, suicidal. Whatever. He found me recently and gave me even more time. Now? I will catch that Farrell off guard and freeze his heart.

~

*D*id I really just write that? What is happening to me? I've abandoned the others and now I'm talking about killing someone.

Someone who will kill me.

I think there's a house nearby. I'll try to find a change of clothing there. I've been on the run for too long in these. I hate crusty clothes! But that's such a stupid luxury to want.

I am ready to use my full powers. Ha ha! Will update after I pay Farrell back for killing Belinda.

~

I wish I had someone to talk to. Instead, I throw all my life down in this diary. I don't even know why. I'll be dead soon. My hands are shaking as I write this. I didn't want to be a murderer, but it would be better than what happened.

Farrell came after me. He knew where I was. He is really good at following my trail. I guess it doesn't hurt that I have to steal everything. I've been running from him through so many places I *don't even know where I am now. I had broken into that house. It seemed like a nice enough split-level home. Kinda reminded me of my own when I was little.*

There was clothing. I cleaned myself best as I could and put it on.

And I feel...good. Awesome. Oh, if I wasn't going to die. Yeah, I was getting to that, wasn't I?

The house I was in made me jump at every move. I expected Farrell or the original owners to walk through the door at any moment. Good thing for me the owners were away for the holiday. I took over their house and started practicing my powers. I needed them more than ever—or so I thought.

I felt almost comfortable. Stupid! I was curling up in bed one night—I love how beds don't freeze. They are just warm and comforting. I only affect water, so I guess a waterbed would be out of the question.

Oh, there I go again, running away from the main issue. Can you tell with my shaky handwriting that I am terrified out of my mind? I was stupid again. I kinda thought Farrell had given up on me. But he's mean. A lot meaner than I thought. He had tracked me to the house because he's something...something evil. He had just followed my tracks.

He showed up when I was sleeping.

It was so dark. The night seemed to bleed through my head. But I heard a noise. I didn't think.

Then Farrell said...He spoke so damned casually. I hate him. I really hate him!

"Hi, sweetheart. Should I join you in bed or should I just kill you?"

I quiver even now. There was so much...evil in his voice. He didn't want me. He never wanted any of us. But he wanted me to think he would...do stuff to me.

It scared the shit out of me. I jumped up and skidded across the floor. There were so many things to hit. I hit a dresser, a lamp, a wall. My head was so sore by the time I managed to get a light on, and the bastard was just standing there, laughing.

"You found out. I wonder how."

It was time, Diary. It was time for me to kill him. I threw my hands out at him and froze him solid. He was encased. I almost laughed at myself. "How about that?" I said.

But there was a reason Farrell always seemed so sure of himself. Bit by bit, my ice, my terrifying and deadly ice—the thing that made my mother turn on me and my father sell me—cracked and disappeared into Farrell. He smiled and said, "Thank you."

I wasn't sure what to do then. That stuff almost killed my mother, but Farrell just laughed it off.

"You are a silly fool. You know about Belinda, don't you?"

I had just nodded. I couldn't speak.

"She controlled fire, you idiot! Which is far more deadly than your silly ice. But I am a Breather. I use your powers against you." Then he blew a kiss at me. I suddenly realized that my powers could be used by my enemy against me. "But more than that, I am a Bloodhound. Now I've got your scent. I can follow you without tracks, without any proof of where you are. It's like you're a beacon, and I will always come right to you." He knelt on the bed and leaned forward, smelling me.

I cringed backward, too afraid to move.

"So, let's make a deal. You come back quietly. You tell the others you saw Belinda out of the facility and living nicely. You assuage the fears you caused. Or you can run. And I can chase you. Oh..." His eyes bored into me. They were slimy. Dark. Angry with me for daring to go against him. "Let me chase you again. It's so useless to have your scent and not chase you. I'd love to feel your fear. Your heart beating so fast and then silenced."

I don't know if I was just being stupid again, but there was a nice fireplace in the room. I vaulted off the bed and picked up a fire poker. I threw it right at him. He tried to duck it, but it grazed his arm. Now that hurt him! Then I ran.

I ran.

I ran.

I ran.

And he keeps finding me. He was right. He had my scent. I don't know how to lose him. I need to end this.

Diary, I have to get a gun. If the fire poker hurt him, a bullet ripping through his chest will tear it to shreds.

The real question is, do I have what it takes to use such a weapon on him—even if he is a monster?

CHAPTER 19

Redmond was so quiet. He must have been going through the same stuff that I had once, so I let him pace and told him I would keep watch. After losing our tail, we broke into a hotel. Redmond had melted the lock, so we had a little bit of a respite. I stared out the window, waiting for any sign of trouble while Redmond was supposed to be sleeping.

Despite Bloodhounds' excellent abilities, distance still stymies them. Digory might be able to follow us, but he had no car. Redmond had pushed our stolen one to the point of no return, so we had a lead on him. Bloodhounds could do whatever they wanted to us, but it wasn't the same with human beings. Otherwise, the whole train could have been destroyed to get to me. No, they had to play nice with humans.

Digory would have to find someone to pick him up or call for some kind of backup. Riders might get involved, but knowing the competitive spirit of these things, I'd bet Digory would continue coming after us alone.

Well, he would keep coming after Redmond. But I

couldn't abandon him. I had lived with my selfish decision to leave my friends behind once. I couldn't do it again, especially with the feelings that were coming from this other Burner. I think I was falling in love with him, but I couldn't trust my feelings.

I also couldn't leave him.

"Redmond," I said, "sleep."

"No way. I can't. That thing…" He trailed off but then looked at me. He sat down on the bed. It looked as if he had enough control over himself to keep the mattress from burning at the very least. "When are you going to tell me?"

"Tell you what?" I asked. My heart leapt into my throat. I couldn't tell him where I had come from, what I had done to get free.

"How do you know so much? Where did you come from?" He stared at me so hard that I felt my resolve weakening. I wanted to touch him, he was so beautiful. From the lines of his perfect face to the hair that I wanted to run my fingers through.

"I can't answer unless I…Can I touch you? I won't kiss you or anything. I just…this attraction is so powerful. Just fingers."

"I know. I was thinking hands. Just holding hands, okay?" Redmond reached out his hand to me. I didn't say no. I sat down next to him, and we held hands. The feeling of uncontrollable need rose out of me again, but I instead turned to his question.

"I was locked up once. I had to escape. I was followed. When we fought, he took my essence. He never stopped. He seemed indefatigable."

"Um, sorry. Never been that hooked on phonics." He gave me a grin and squeezed my hand.

"It means untiring." I let myself settle more into the bed. I knew I should be on the lookout, but that question hurt me, and right now Redmond was giving me comfort of the kind I had never known before. "But I needed a bigger word than that. I was hunted for years before I found the sewer and realized that Farrell couldn't find me there. I've been hunted by both kinds of Breathers: Riders and Bloodhounds. Breathers in general can know that a Burner is among a group of people, but a Bloodhound knows what you're feeling, where you are, everything your body's doing. After Farrell's death, they knew I was dangerous, so the sewer saved me."

Redmond didn't answer for a few minutes. He just scooted closer to where our hips touched. Amazing, amazing touch!

"You killed him." It wasn't a question.

"I had to. I couldn't stay in the sewers. I needed food. And you know what else."

Redmond slid closer to me. Now our legs were touching as well. "And that's what we have to do now."

"They're monsters." Oops, my hand—the one that wasn't touching Redmond wanted to get in on this whole touching thing. It reached up as if beyond my control to put my fingers under Redmond's ear. He leaned into me and sighed. "All of them," I continued desperately as if to ignore my hand's wanderings. "They have powers too. And they never ever stop."

Redmond pulled me to him. "If they're monsters, why do you feel so bad?"

My eyes opened inches away from his face. My breath caught at his beauty so up close.

"Yes, I can tell. Your guilt radiates off you. Like mine does when I think about that poor family I killed. But they were innocents. These things are murderers."

I pushed my lip out. I felt like crying, but I didn't want to drop ice on Redmond. He was so close. I didn't want things icy between us. "I still don't like it. Killing is wrong. I don't know much. I just know that no one should bring a life to an end. If we have all these extra powers, doesn't that mean we have extra responsibilities? It's easy…so easy to kill."

His eyes gazed at my face and I knew he was thinking about what had happened when he and his father got into the accident. "But if it's kill or be killed, then I vote for kill."

"You don't understand," I whispered. "And we are getting way too close."

"I know," Redmond said, but he leaned down for a kiss.

Then the hotel window exploded.

CHAPTER 20

iary,
Excuse my writing. I'm in a one-bed hotel room, waiting. I have a gun. I don't want to tell you how I got it. Sheesh. I just read that last line. Who else can I tell the whole truth? Okay, time to confess. Wait...

'm back. I heard a noise. I don't like this place. It's better than the sewer, but not by much. This dismal little room smells. It's dark all the time. And there is so much noise out there. Farrell could be out there. Every pound of the bass next door makes my heart beat in time. Okay, I've got to stop breathing so hard. The cigarette smoke is choking me enough without breathing it in. One second.

ack again. Had to look out the tiny window with the sheer curtain. Some boozers are singing out a song near my window. Irritating, but kind of like birds that flee trees when hunters come. They wouldn't be so jovial if they saw Farrell. No human could be. Their stupid song is as good as an alarm if it's silenced.

Okay, back to the gun. I think it's bad of me. I am going to kill tonight. I'm going to shoot a bullet right through Farrell's heart. I am so sick of running, being afraid every time I leave my home for food. Knowing that Farrell will be on my heels. I anticipate—I yearn for the sight of his blood bursting out of his chest. But I feel guilty about stealing! Yes, stealing. I froze the lock on a gun shop, and it was easy after that to do the same to the safe. I got a rifle. It's propped under my neck now. Ammo. Money. I could have checked into the best hotel, wallowed in luxury as I waited. Eaten room service. I want chocolate!

But I...What a stupid thing to be! Guilty about stealing but not about the idea of murdering a living creature. Maybe because Daddy got it into my head that stealing was wrong. He didn't teach me the same about murder. Maybe it was all those shows he watched where someone was murdered as part of the plot.

Shit. Shit. Shit. The drunken musicians have quieted. Gotta go. If I survive, I'll write tonight. Now instead of later. When I'm free.

~

can't...I did it. I have to write this out. Have to. Stop shaking, hands! Okay. Okay. Okay. Farrell came. He slid under my window like the night. The people outside found better places to be. A primal instinct to be away from a predator that could rip your face off.

The jackal surprised me. All my waiting and he just popped his head up in front of the window. Talk about jump scares! He grinned and tapped on my window. Tap, tap, tap.

I couldn't control myself. I jumped and scrambled backward. I dropped my gun. I suck! I was waiting for him and I dropped my freaking weapon!

I heard his laugh. His sickening, "I'll hurt you the worst way" kind of laugh. His tapping became banging.

Now he was the one who totally sucked. His attempts to scare me only gave me the chance to grab my rifle again. I had no clue on how to load it. But I'm smart. I had to be. Bullets go there. Aim. Stop the freaking shaking hands!

The window shattered. Farrell was strong. Then he stuck his head in. The minimal light glinted against the silver in his eyes. His thick lips were twisted into a smile, like this was a game.

"Hello, sweetheart. Want to go home? This chase has been fun." He started climbing through the window, one long leg, and then the other. Then he saw the gun in my hand. He cocked his head. Amused.

"Little girl, you aren't going to use that on me, are you? You're no murderer. You're fast. Smart even. You want to survive. Well, you will. You have time. One more year. But more importantly, we need you to return. Maybe we'll let you graduate at another time. It could be arranged."

He was talking. Diary, I don't know why. But I started asking questions. I wanted to know why Belinda died. Why we all were going to.

"What do you do to us? I thought we were safe. But you..." My hands slipped around the gun. Butterfingers. I shouldn't have had a gun.

My question made him angry. I wasn't doing what he wanted, which was to beg for my life and give in to anything he demanded.

"Well, I want two things. One, I've told you. The other—" His eyes roved over me. "—can be worked out."

I couldn't answer, Diary. He had freaked me out. He was in my hotel room, just lounging against the wall. Picking up the magazines that had been left there and flipping through them. His extremely long legs stretched against the floor like a spider's.

"Belinda fought, you know. She burned off the stuff we used in seconds. She had grown just too powerful. Strange, she burnt out before she even was used. The extraction killed her because there just wasn't enough left."

I had no idea what he was talking about, but I got a sort of sick pleasure that whatever it was Farrell wanted was frustrated when he tried with Belinda. She died a hero. She saved me.

As Farrell advanced toward me, I knew if I didn't do something soon, her sacrifice would be in vain.

"You have time, sweetie. Don't waste it. Don't make me kill you now. Don't be selfish. There are other Burners at our facility. You know that. If you come back, they won't fear the future for the short remnant they have left. You will be a hero."

Forgive me, Diary, but I considered it. No more running. Back in comfort. Knowing when my next meal would be, confined in the suit that kept my powers away. I could eat normally again. And maybe Farrell would honor this agreement. He probably would. Me coming back and preventing the rest from being afraid would be worth it to delay...Well, whatever it was they did to us. I didn't know. Farrell wasn't sharing.

But I couldn't. All I could think about was that hero word. The one that sacrifices for others. But what was I gaining by going back? I would continue a lie. A lie that we all were okay, that we graduated to a better life. Instead, they'd all die, like sheep to the slaughter.

In the next minute, everything went crazy. He lunged at me. Like he didn't really think I'd come willingly, or he didn't want me to. I pulled back and fell to the ground. I held onto the gun. But I didn't point it at him. He had my leg.

I can still feel his grip, even now. I'm back in my sewer. Why, you ask? Aren't I free? Ha! Diary, you naïve idiot. Oh, yes, I'm free from Farrell, but the rest will know I killed him. They might not know my scent, but they're out there.

Oops, again, I'm going away from what happened. Like I said, I had fallen. He grabbed my leg. I kicked out wildly and hit him in the chin. He turned, like, demonic. His whole face snarled and he punched me in the face. Man, it hurt! I think he split my lip.

I don't know why, but I wiggled and my ice ripped out of me. I wanted to attack. So, blades. They cut him. Blood poured from his face. I think I screamed. I mean that must have been what made Farrell so excited.

All I can remember now is that Farrell reached out with his hands. They encircled my throat. I pulled the gun up. I fired.

Blammo! Into his heart. I killed him. His blood poured out all over me.

Did you know, Diary, that when Breathers die, they send out a signal? Yeah, I didn't. But as his eyes faded out, his mouth opened in a high-pitched wail and I knew. This was only the beginning.

I ran. Again. Maybe I'll write more later. But not tonight. Tonight, I will wash with dirty water from the sewer to get the blood off. I smeared this page already.

I killed Farrell. He no longer has my scent.

But the rest are after me. They'll track me to the last place Farrell was. Out there. My life is now hiding.

Oh, Belinda, where is the world you promised? It's not meant for me.

As I lay my pencil down, I can only say one more thing. I'm so sorry to the rest of my Burner friends. But it's me now. Everything is me. Surviving.

This is who I am.

CHAPTER 21

It was a good thing we were already so close together. I managed to throw up my ice shield and take the brunt of the debris that hit us like shrapnel. Redmond's eyes were wide next to mine.

"Go!" I yelled, and we jumped up. The roof was gone. The shards were falling in ashy clumps.

Outside, there were two of them. Digory was standing next to a black motorcycle, on the back of which was a huge mountain of a man. Metal shined under the half-moon in the black sky.

Digory swept his hands through his long hair nodded when he saw me looking at him.

A Rider. A freaking Rider.

"What's that?" Redmond asked. His fire burned over his body, but he wasn't throwing any yet. He was learning caution. How nice.

"That's a Rider. It's how he blew up our room."

I reached out and took his hand. His fire didn't harm me. If this had been another time, another place, and I wasn't in mortal danger, I would have felt happy holding his hand.

What the freak kind of spell did we Burners have over others?

Illogically silly, I hoped Redmond felt the same about me.

My fragmented mind obsessed with his hand—his perfect hand—even as Digory gestured to the Rider. The Rider knelt on the ground and pushed some kind of large-barreled gun onto his shoulder. His sunglasses gleamed the same as his extra white teeth.

Redmond's hands moved.

"Don't!" I cried as we stumbled backward. The smoke entered my lungs, choking me. Then it disappeared inside—a benefit of being a Burner. Nothing lives long inside my body. I pulled his arm as we jumped through the shell that was once the wall. Then we ran.

I cursed myself as we did. The hotel was nearly empty. We had broken into a room that had no neighbors. As much as we tried to avoid humans, they would have been a protective wall in their own way.

The hallways were cramped with chunks of plaster, fallen from the beating the place was taking. I could hear the walls quaking as the Rider fired again and again.

"Don't attack them." We took one breath under a reinforced archway on the way out of the building. "It'll do nothing against the Rider. We need a lot more for that."

Redmond surprised me with a laugh. "Laoni, I heard somewhere that you don't attack the bullet, you attack the hand holding the gun. I was planning something."

I felt my face freeze. Oh, I hoped his plan wouldn't get us both killed.

His eyes shot behind us to where Digory and the Rider were slowly gaining on us. Both had normal guns now, waiting for the moment when they could take aim. They ducked and dodged falling material and hot walls. Just like

Redmond and I, though, neither needed gas masks. They could breathe in the ash just like we could.

"That's what I thought," Redmond muttered.

"What is?" I asked and sidled the wall, trying to get out of the sight of either gun.

"They don't want to get burned."

I shook my head. I felt like throwing up. We were going to die and Redmond was acting like this was one big game.

To my surprise, Redmond brought me close, like he was going to kiss me. Staring me eye to eye. My thoughts were confined chaos again. Even with two killers aiming to wound and the slow fall of black ash around me, I was getting lost.

"You can't burn, right?"

I leaned up toward him. My lips were aching for his touch. "I'm the Burner, remember?"

"I thought so."

Then he drew me in for a kiss as he snapped his fingers. I didn't exactly know where the plume of fire went. I just knew it got extremely warm around us. I didn't care. Even as flames of fire licked my ankles, I licked Redmond's lip. My body craved him. His touch. His entire being. His fingers swept into my hair. I clutched the back of his head, drawing him ever closer.

He lifted me up to get better access and shoved my back into the wall.

Oh, no wall. It was gone. We tumbled to the ground, still connected. But the drop got to us. My head ached from hitting the ground. Redmond rubbed his knee where it had banged into a metal pipe.

A metal pipe? From what?

I finally could look around. I stood up with my mouth gaping, still excited from that kiss. The world was a fiery hell. Everything was on fire. The hotel had been a large rectangular C shape. The end we had been in was in ruins. I could see the Rider and Digory engulfed in fire. They were running.

"How?"

"That's not my fire." He gave me a sheepish grin. My heart leapt as I saw that his lips were swollen from my kisses. It made my body react, and I really wished we hadn't been caught in a fiery building.

"I mean, sure," he said as we started walking. The fire trucks would arrive soon. We couldn't be seen. "My fire would have just been magically absorbed or something. But when it hits wood and spreads, I guess it stops being something the Breathers can inhale. Didn't you notice that they were avoiding the hot metal? The falling debris? They're far from immortal."

Well, I knew that! Hadn't I killed Farrell? But I had never thought the very elements of the world around us could aid us if they were just removed from our direct control. Redmond had saved us. We were making good time, but we had no car. I wasn't sure if Digory was dead or not. I hoped he was. We couldn't exactly stick around looking over his burning body, though.

"What now?" I asked.

Redmond laughed again. He was pretty jovial for someone who could have killed two Breathers so easily. Far from how I felt when I did it. Farrell still haunted me. Sometimes when I slept at night, I would picture his face when he saw the bullet enter his flesh. I wondered if Digory on fire would be added to the nightly arsenal against me.

"What are you laughing about?" I asked.

"I don't know. I've got a clue. But let's just say it's the adrenaline. Or maybe it's the fact that we just figured out how to get rid of these guys. Maybe because you're asking me what to do now, but you're the one in charge, honeybunch."

I wrinkled my nose but fought a smile. Life finally being not so life-or-death wasn't bad at all. No one was following us. I checked a half a dozen times as we turned onto another street filled with homes that blocked us from the main street. Digory wouldn't be coming after us any time soon. He had all those burns to take care of. And Redmond had just called *me* honeybunch.

I bristled because I thought I should. "Don't call me that."

"Okay, sweetheart."

I stuck my tongue out at him.

"I get it." But he was still smiling, looking crazily sane for someone who almost killed two people. "I've got an idea. And I want you to just go along with it. How long do we have until those two come again?"

I didn't know. I had destroyed the ones that came after me. I had never burned them. "Hours, maybe. They still need to get treatment. Digory is determined, but…"

Redmond nodded. His whole face was beaming. "Great! We've got time. Laoni, would you mind going to get us some food. It doesn't matter what. I saw a store around the corner."

Now I was really confused. "Um, no money. Stealing is the only way."

Redmond just fluttered his hands to dismiss that. "Then go ahead. Get anything. I'll burn it anyway, so…"

"Where are you going?" I was too suspicious. I didn't know if this was just a way to get away from me. Was he going to take that car and drive away? I would. But then again, *he* was the one who could be hunted.

"Won't tell." A mischievous air was around him. What was going on?

But he wouldn't answer, so I was sent off. I snuck

around the corner, and sure enough, there was a store. Thankfully one that had closed early. I froze the glass and busted a hole. Redmond said it didn't matter, but I pretended. Pretended it did. I got some steak, sparkling water. Ice cream. The last was for him. I wondered if it would help at all. By the time I was done, Redmond was picking me up again. Ah, crap…

"You didn't!" I squealed.

But he did. He was wearing a suit. A rich coal-black that made his blond hair shimmer under the streetlights. Hair that he had combed backward with some kind of gel. He had flowers. He gestured to a table in front of a closed café, and nobody was on the street.

"I thought it was time for our first date," he said.

I closed my eyes. He was truly insane. This was *not* happening. I still took the flowers, smelled them, and then quickly got them away from me. They didn't need my frost.

I put down the food and stared at him. I felt shyer than ever before. "Why?"

"That kiss, sweets."

"Again, with the nicknames…"

"I thought it fitting. It was obvious when you almost made me forget the building was falling around us."

I flicked the table. It was metal with lots of holes, so I could see the sidewalk underneath. "What was obvious? That we were totally entranced by each other?"

"No. It's obvious that…I'm in love with you."

"That's what I was afraid of. Redmond, it was just one kiss."

Redmond laughed and pulled my hand forward, trapping it in his. "That was no kiss. That was a life-affirming embrace. Things need to change. I know it's fast."

"Too fast."

"But things like that happen. Look at Romeo and Juliet."

I gagged. "Really? That's the best you can come up with? They both died!"

Redmond tipped my chin upward to look into my eyes. "We won't. That kiss wasn't just great. It was protection. I protected you. And I felt more human than ever before. The last time I brought my powers up to protect people, I killed them all. That changed in your arms."

I pushed the ice cream forward. My tone was a bit snappish when I said, "Try the ice cream. Will it melt or burn?"

He grinned and opened up the container. He scooped it into his mouth. It did melt, so fast it made steam escape from his lips. He still said, "Mmmm. Now, what should I call you?"

I glared at him. I snapped the steak onto the table from its plastic wrapping. "Can you cook it? Frozen raw meat tastes worse than frozen cooked meat."

Redmond rubbed a finger over the meat and made it brown. I was chewing it before he continued.

"So, what endearment can I call you? My dad called my mom love muffin before...the dark times. Before the empire."

I shook my head.

Redmond groaned. "*Star Wars*. Come on! You have to have seen *Star Wars*. If not, the first thing we'll do as boyfriend and girlfriend will be to watch it."

I couldn't seem to function. "I've seen it. It's just...You don't get it. I mean..."

Redmond took my hand again. "This is real, Laoni. I know it."

"Coming from the pessimist?"

He shook his head. He was silent as we both ate. The steak burned into charcoal as he put it into his mouth. Tendrils of smoke spilled out and touched the night sky under the glowing lights. We finished our food before he spoke again. I think he was just enjoying my presence—

enjoying me. I thought this was complicated before. But that kiss had changed everything for him. For me? I was still on the fence. I was the only one he could touch, and I was gorgeous. How could I trust both convenience and beauty?

Finally, we finished our meal and started walking. We didn't have the ability to stay in one place for long. Hunted people don't have that luxury. We still needed to find somewhere to go. Somewhere to be safe. But for right now, this was way more important. I couldn't believe Redmond was so positive now.

"I'm not a pessimist anymore. The kiss changed everything. Laoni, that was incredible. I had just thought to keep you close. If the fire hurt you, I might have been able to draw it off. But then…I can't even. My lips are still tingling. I need you, Laoni. And maybe you didn't notice, but we won! And together, I'm starting to believe we can accomplish anything."

I dropped his hand. My feet walked faster. "Because you're a Burner! Because I'm a Burner. We can't stop the way we feel. It's all part of our stupid makeup. I desire you more than anything ever, even staying alive. I'd die just for a touch from you."

Redmond caught up with me. One touch from his finger on my shoulder and I stopped. I didn't look at him. I didn't want him to see the ice ball tears that were already touching my chin.

"You can't be sure of that."

I couldn't respond. He was infuriating! I had told him again and again how there was no *choice* in our relationship.

"Come on," he cajoled. Stupid silly me turned around, exposing my tears. So much for pride.

He caught the little pieces of ice, but they melted against his fiery skin. "Don't cry. This is good, not bad. I know it."

"Faster," I urged instead of a normal response. I didn't

need to cry all day. "We can steal a car—you can, I mean. Then we can be further north. Once we hit the water line, we'll be able to figure out the *Freedom* ship."

He took my hand. I didn't pull away. I should have pulled away.

"Let's finish this topic as we walk then. We don't have to run." His thumb worked my knuckle. The warmth was something I could never have understood. It wasn't right, but it was the best thing in the world.

"What topic?" We crossed the street. My feet were starting to hurt from walking. It really reminded me of the past. "You want me because I'm a Burner. I want you because you're a Burner. If we get together, we'll always ask the same question. Do we love each other, or is it just Burner attraction? I don't want that."

Redmond brought my hand up to his lips. He breathed hot air on my knuckles as he kissed them slowly and methodically. "Reason one, I think you're incredible. Surviving all these years even with those *creatures* after you."

"Reason?" I swallowed my own tongue. I liked his mouth on my knuckles too, too much. I didn't know how I could speak.

"My reasons for liking you, Wonder Woman."

I bit my lip to stop the smile. I hated those stupid names he was calling me! Why encourage him? "Okay, fine. And I like the fact that you are fearless. Is that it? Because I've got news for you! We're drawn to each other's beauty."

Dawn came. It crept over the buildings until it made everything glow. The sun hit us both in the face. Redmond brought up his hand. Not to shade his eyes but to shade mine. I swatted him away. "Stop that!"

"Reason two, I like the fact that you will discuss books with me. You like my snacks."

I couldn't help it. "I like those things too. We'd never argue about what to do if we were, you know, a couple."

"Reason three. You are beautiful, yes. Totally goddess like. But the first time I felt like I wanted to kiss you was when you made that ice wall that got us away from Digory. That's why. The light in your eyes drew me. The passion in you. I have never met a girl like you. If our world were different, I'd have asked you out. I would have made a big deal of it. You know how you've seen those crazy videos of marriage proposals? Well, I would have done a flash mob or something like that.

"Ha! You scoff. You didn't know me…before. I wasn't as bad as I am now. Sure, I saw bad in life, but I was always passionate. It was the death. All the death that I caused. But this time, because you were near me, I didn't kill anyone. I controlled something I thought would kill me someday. I was wrong. It's because of you.

"Laoni, you are a magnificent girl. Special in more ways than one. You don't see the change you've made in me. But I do. I don't have a flash mob. So, this is the best thing I can do. Will you go out with me?"

I held his hand so tight I was afraid I'd break it. I would have had him completely covered in ice if he hadn't been a Burner. I knew what my brain said. Redmond didn't understand the appeal. He was new to this world. Everything he wanted could be attributed to that insane allure we both had.

But my heart was stolen away by his allure. And I didn't care. I'd crash later as long as I could soar now. "When we can, we'll have dinner and a movie," I said.

Redmond cheered. The idiot cheered out loud, sending a yodel down the street.

"Shut up!" I hissed. "This could all end in heartbreak. Maybe I'll disappoint you."

Redmond rolled his gorgeous gray eyes. "Laoni, does

everything have to work in the future for you to do something now?"

I couldn't answer him. The sun had come up, but the sky was covered in a dense, cold gray. Snow was coming. The air around was becoming cold. Icy. I could feel the temperature dropping. A special playground for me. I didn't know what it'd be like for Redmond. Suddenly, I was very happy about the decision I'd made.

"What will snow do to you?" I asked.

Redmond shrugged, still looking at me with the smile that made his face look extremely silly. "Never had the misfortune to find out. Probably just evaporate. Maybe we should get a car."

I was still thinking about the last person's car we stole. I wondered if they had insurance or if they were just stretching their paycheck week to week. I wondered if they would lose their job because of no car.

"Laoni, share. Please. That's the good thing about having a boyfriend."

I shot him a look. "We've only had one date, you know."

"Yeah. So?"

With a sigh, I told him. We passed several possible cars as I told him my worries and fears. Well, regarding the car. We would have been walking for years if I had let him know all my problems. The snow I could feel coming had started sprinkling. I hadn't encountered a lot of snow, but sometimes a storm would blow through where I was running, and it looked like one was blowing now.

Redmond was right in a way. The snow did evaporate on him. But a new aspect of our existence was revealed.

It made Redmond itch. Like seriously itch. Every time a flake landed, he wiggled like a cat. The poor boy was in ultimate discomfort. And I was too. Because the snow made me itch, too? No, because his body movements made me itch.

I was growing more and more distracted by this new guy in my life. This hadn't happened before. Not that I'd ever had much opportunity. The only men after me weren't interested in a pleasant encounter. Farrell hadn't wanted me at all. And the Rider way back when…I didn't like thinking about him.

I had barely escaped. My journal for him wasn't even in full sentences. He had gotten the closest.

"We need to steal a car, now," I said as he wiggled his strong torso. I could see his overdeveloped pecs straining against his shirt. I wanted to touch them. I wished *I* was what his shirt was straining against.

"But you did raise some good points," he muttered. Another snowflake hit him on the back of the neck. "I never think about the people I steal from. But I…How many did I hurt? I've hacked into bank accounts. I've taken most of the money. But what if it had been for a rent payment? What if…"

Redmond had caught my disease. He expelled theory after theory, making even my imagination lack in comparison.

Suddenly I couldn't take it anymore. "Stop!" I said.

"Why?" He had the saddest face I had seen as of yet. He wasn't holding my hand. Like he didn't deserve the joy that gave him.

"Life and death take precedence over problems. Those people, hey, yeah, they have monetary problems. But they're still alive. We won't be if we don't run and keep running. Or eat. Or sleep. Or whatever."

Redmond wiggled his shoulders in irritation. "Yeah. But you brought it up."

The snow was increasing. It evaporated in a halo around Redmond and settled on me, making me look bigger than I was.

I passed a Ferrari and stopped. I reached out and pointed.

Seconds later the locks froze. I jiggled the latch and the door popped open. "A Ferrari, Redmond. Anyone who has this probably wouldn't have money troubles if they lost it. More than likely it's insured for a whole hell of a lot. Get in. Get out of the snow. Life or death. If more Breathers come, we die."

He regarded me for a few seconds. I could see the wall he put over his memories slide into place again. The stuff that kept his guilt at bay. The stuff I had pulled away just to whine about my own conscience. I had made a choice. We both did. That was what we did. We had to. Something up there forced us to live the way we were. I wouldn't bring up my own problems again. Never. Not if they would sway Redmond.

It was with that thought that I realized.

I was falling in love with him. The allure thing had totally affected my mind, so much that I was starting to believe I loved him just for him and not the manipulation of his power. But I had liked too many people like me. I had ended up betraying all of them. How would Redmond be any different?

But I ignored that. He was suddenly more important than my own problems. That's why I'd keep them at bay and not let them affect the both of us.

CHAPTER 22

*O*kay, here we go, Diary. I gotta talk about Riders.

I'm not sure of the requirements to become a Rider, but I think one is that they have to be ugly. I've seen some very unattractive bikers, but when it comes to Riders, they seem to work at it. Maybe it's their line of work. Scars are prevalent. Facial scars reaching from noses to brow. Scars up their arms. No tattoos. You'd think they'd want tattoos, but it's almost like they're against them.

Maybe the ugliness comes from within. They like the hunt too much. Farrell liked the hunt, too, but he wasn't as manic about it. Like, Farrell did it for a point, a greater goal. Riders do what they do, and more, for fun. No reason behind it.

I don't know where they get the machines, and their bikes are far from normal. Sleek black metal that reaches out to grab the rims. Shiny steering wheels. The seat isn't padded at all. It's metal itself. It's like the Riders want to feel the heat of the bike under them. Some kind of love affair. The bikes make the Riders terrifying on their own, coming at you like some demon from hell.

But Riders know machines more than anything else. Riders could win world wars with their deep knowledge of weapons. But the Riders only use that knowledge for the goal of hunting Burners.

Their skin is thicker than normal skin. I know. It takes more than a bullet to take them out. It takes ten. One after another. In the same spot. It's a very good thing the Runners hate working alongside them.

Let me think. They're fast, agile. Mean sons of guns. Or sons of something. I don't know what mother could love these things. They're all male. Or at least they all look male. Runners can be either, but Riders come in one package. Mean. Big. Burly. Shoulders the size of an ox. Huge, long faces with different facial features. Some wear beards. Some have piercings. Some are really flat-faced.

Their eyes are purple. All the exact same color. No irises or pupils. Just a purple emptiness. Their thighs are big, round cords of muscle. I could fit my waist inside just one.

Did I mention that they are mean?

I haven't seen them desire or aim for anything but the destruction and torture of Burners. Riders do nothing but Ride toward their next victim. They don't sleep or eat as long as prey is in their way.

They do have these desires. I've seen them sleep. They also have other desires. They are into my allure—Burners' allures—more so than even the other Breathers I've seen. And they like pain.

Okay, fine, I'm just judging on the one Rider I've met. I haven't had the bad luck to encounter more than one. And I left that bastard trapped under the ice.

Yes, it seems they do need to breathe.

His massive fists pounding against my ice as I continued to layer it upward, using all the water in the lake for my arsenal, is burned into my memory. Those purple eyes, panicked and scared.

Good. That evened the score between us. Though he hadn't touched me. And I did end his pathetic life.

I hate Riders. They can come up on you without you knowing. Their bikes are faster than any speedy car.

I never want to see one again. Ever.

Damn it. I hate getting like this. I just want to talk about things in here, not babble. I want to leave something I can look back on and remember that these demons have weaknesses.

I have killed Farrell and a Rider.

Score.

CHAPTER 23

I had to admit, I liked Ferraris. They were fast. I kinda wished I knew how to drive so I could take her out. Redmond was a great driver, though. He knew almost instinctively how to drive it.

It was early and, thanks to the snow, things were closed, so the traffic on the highway dwindled. We saw no cops, which was a boon. I didn't want to hurt any humans. But I would if it meant them or me. I had to keep reminding myself that in normal circumstances, I could have morals. Ethics. But if I was facing death, then I had to do anything and everything in my power to stay alive. Being good to other human beings only came when one was at peace. All was fair in war.

"You're quiet," Redmond noted. Sometimes it was nice to have someone else to run with. Sometimes it was a pain in the ass. Redmond knowing my moods could be a benefit. But it was irritating. It was hard enough to keep all these thoughts inside my head. I didn't need them spilling over to Redmond, where they would regain strength.

"Hey, it's fun. Go faster." I shot him a grin. He pushed the pedal down. The dark road underneath the tires shot toward us with bullet speed. I barely blinked and road signs disappeared behind us.

"Hey, my girl, come lean on my shoulder," Redmond said. He sounded careless. Free. What I wanted to be. And we were on the road to freedom. We'd find that ship. No Breathers were on our tail.

I did as he asked and slipped over the best I could and leaned on his shoulder. For a split second, I felt happy. Careless.

And wouldn't you know my luck? That was when the Rider pulled up beside Redmond's window.

CHAPTER 24

*D*iary,

    I'm scared. Really scared. I didn't know. Didn't think. More. There were always more. Farrell had my scent, but he left a trace which others followed. As soon as I relax, I have to fear. One caught up with me. I'm under a bridge. I hope it's enough. The Rider is here. He drives back and forth over me. Does he know where I am? My hands hurt, I'm clutching this pen so tightly.

If he knows where I am...

I hear the motor. It's coming closer.

Above me, I hear his boots.

He's talking to me. He knows where I am! No. Maybe I could—

I'm back. Maybe. He's got me in a room. Only one door, no windows. It still hurts where he punched me. Still hurts where he threw me over the back of his bike. And the road, the rocks hitting me.

    This is my goodbye. I know I'm dead. The Rider hasn't called for backup. We're alone. He's outside right now. I hear sharpening. Shick. Shick. Shick.

Fun. He said we'd have fun. But will he kill me?

What is he sharpening? Sorry. Be strong. I won't cry. I won't scream. No satisfaction for him.

Diary, I'll try and focus. Keep it together. He told me what he planned to do. Can't repeat it here. Too scared. Can't think. I wonder where my mom is. I wonder if Dad ever thinks of me the way I think of him...

I hear him. Laughing. He's calling for me. I'll tell you what he says. Need to shut down. Stop feeling. I can relay what he says. No worries.

"I like you at this age even though I've never gotten the chance to be alone with one before. I have to say, you're beautiful."

The door opens. I see the glint of the knife from the light behind him. Keep it together. There is a kitchen behind him. This is his home. So, Riders have homes. They have the need for shelter.

"You're ignoring me," he says. Of course. I'm writing. I can't believe he doesn't take you away from me.

Okay. I can't repeat his words. He's crude. He uses swears like they're going out of style. Yes, yes, I get how many different ways you can eff me up. He's starting to irritate me.

Anger! Ah, there you are, old friend. Fear is going away.

"When I'm finished—" He's still talking. Great. I get a villain that won't shut up. "—I'll hand you over to them and still get my reward. And I get a night with you I won't forget. Memories. I love them. Almost as good as the act."

He's close to me. He's breathing over my head. I amw writinga as fast asi Can now. I have to finish. He's goingggg to ccccut me. Damnmmit. My hands are shaking.

I hate him!

He's reaching ootu now—

～

*O*h, Diary,

I'm saved. I'm safe. I'm free. I have gone back to my wonderful sewer. It's beautiful. Okay, the design is. I love the little tiles. But it's even more beautiful for what it means. I'm safe here again. No Breather will find me. I have to duck out and get food, but I have a home again.

Not like my old one.

Great, I'm smiling now. Not in a funny ha ha way, but in a wry way. My home isn't the one with my parents. It was the facility. With my friends. But it's gone now. Belinda is dead, and the others will be someday. I left them.

My smile's gone. I think I'm crying.

Oh right. The Rider. I started this to write about what happened. My hands still shake, but I can manage.

He had the knife. He had it raised, brought it down. Did I tell you I was angry? Because I was. Somehow, I wanted to cut him like he wanted to cut me. I didn't even think about what had happened with Farrell. I could have made a horrible mistake. But I wanted to hurt him.

For scaring me. For what he wanted to do to me. So, I did something I never thought about before. I made my ice into a weapon. Oh, not as the blade that I had with Farrell. I made a real ice sword and I thrust it into his gut. The Rider dropped the knife and looked at me with shock. It was enough for me to get away.

My anger was gone, but the sword didn't stop the Rider.

I ran out of his stupid house, right in the middle of suburbia, like he was a normal guy. It was midnight. There were no stars overhead. And as usual, I didn't really know how cold it was.

The Rider came after me. A sword through his stomach wasn't enough.

And I had no more. I didn't have the strength to do it again. The fear was back. How could I stop him if a sword couldn't? Maybe they were immortal.

Maybe I should just die and end this stupid chase.

But I don't know. I can't explain it. I did want to give up more than anything. I heard the roar of the motorcycle behind me. I could almost feel his breath on me again.

As I write this, I feel like an idiot. The clouds overhead parted and a lone star shined through. I thought it was, get this, a message from the heavens telling me to keep going, like I wasn't truly alone. Someone was watching over me and didn't want me to give up.

It sounds stupid now. Just like Belinda's fairy tale.

But it fooled me. I sped up. Just across the black ground, I saw a glimmer of that same star in the lake. A lake! A whole bunch of water that I could freeze. I ran right onto it.

The stupid Rider followed. His bike had trouble getting its grip on the slick surface that I left behind.

So, I guess my powers were complete. No longer could I control them. When water touched me, even through shoes, it froze.

"Stop running!" the Rider screamed behind me. He was angry. Maybe it was my imagination, but I could smell his blood. His wound still wept. "I'll keep you!" he added. "For myself. For a long time. I won't get my money. I'll just enjoy your growing up."

I stopped. The water around me was frozen. The lake, though, stayed warm. I turned around and let his motorcycle catch up. I felt the ice under him. He was so sure it would keep him safe.

But the ice was my ally. Not his.

"You won't touch me. You'll never have fun. But I'm starting to get a taste for Breather blood."

I guess I was being melodramatic, Diary. I was just sick of him. I brought my hand into a fist, and the ice shifted away from under his wheels. In seconds, his bike went under, and he with it. Then I put the ice back.

He swam upward, kicking his legs. His bike was long gone.

Crack! The ice cracked under his punches. I reached out for more ice. Layer after layer.

He struggled and pounded. I could almost feel it in my bones.

He was a living creature, and he cared about surviving as much as the next person. But so did I. Not just existing for me. As I well knew now, life wasn't the only thing to lose in this world. There was freedom, comfort, and happiness.

The Rider wanted all of them from me.

I didn't stop. I slid sheet after sheet over his face. He realized on the sixth one, he wasn't going to escape. His mouth opened as he lost his breath. I kept going.

I buried him. Then he sank. As water permeated his body and stole his oxygen, he went away. I only saw his eyes. Afraid.

Like I had been.

I crawled to the side of the lake and collapsed. I think I slept for two days. It had taken all my energy to trap him. Oh, and a whole lake of my friend the water.

I had taken two lives.

Diary! I have killed two men. I think I don't care. What does that say about me? Am I a monster now? Or maybe I always was. Who else can control ice? From now on, all the others I meet...they will be gone. And I will be the only Burner left. And there are other Riders. Other Breathers. They won't stop until they kill us all.

Kill or be killed.

I would kill.

CHAPTER 25

Redmond didn't need any encouragement to slam down the accelerator to full speed. The Rider's grin had shaken him. It wasn't the same Rider, though. I don't know what happened to that one.

"Where did he come from?" Redmond asked.

"My guess? We killed one of the Breathers."

"I did, you mean."

"Whatever. One of them must have let out a death wail."

"I don't wanna know!" Redmond said, keeping his eyes on our tail. "These things don't stop, do they? They just keep coming!"

"Story of my life," I said. "No biggie." But it was a biggie. Just when I thought I could be safe, something worse had to happen. "Speed up."

"Pedal's already to the metal," he grunted back.

It didn't matter. The Riders were too fast. It's how one caught me so long ago. But to my surprise, the Rider fell behind. That made no sense. He wouldn't give up. Everything in their arsenal could…

"Weave!" I screamed as a missile skidded across the ground, shot from the underside of the Rider's bike. He had slowed down to get a better shot.

Another one!

Redmond was a great driver. He threw the car sideways and shot back to the other side. He wasn't giving the Rider a good target. Redmond kept one eye on the road in front, all attention on the bike behind. But there was nowhere we could go. The Rider would speed up if we went toward residential areas. He wouldn't want the humans involved.

I watched the Rider behind us. He had stopped shooting missiles. Suddenly, his bike changed. It grew, roaring over the road. Then he sped up. He was going to overtake us.

The roof of the car obscured it, but I knew what he had done. His two wheels had become four to straddle our car, and up above was the main body. He easily matched our pace no matter how fast Redmond drove.

Then...

Bzzzzzzzzz.

He was cutting through our roof!

Redmond and I shared panicked eyes. I couldn't let the Rider grab Redmond. Concern for my own safety was far away. I was terrified for Redmond now. This Rider could hurt me so much more than the last one was capable of. It was hard having someone to protect.

Snow sped toward the windshield like a wall of ice. I could stop this. Easily.

But I hesitated.

Redmond looked at the widening hole. His face tightened. "Let's see how well you do with your nice bike on fire," he growled. Fire exploded through the roof, but nothing happened.

"That engine isn't exploding!" Redmond yelled and changed lanes, trying to throw the Breather off the top.

"Their machines aren't normal."

"I hate this!" Redmond yelled. He pounded on the steering wheel, filling the car with noise. "I can't fry him. Can't bring fire to him. What the hell is the point of abilities if you can't even use them?"

I could use mine. I could show Redmond my monster. As I stared at the side of his head. My decision was easy.

"Redmond, I'll be a little exhausted after this. Keep driving north. Keep a lookout for the mountain that looks like a lady."

"Why?" Redmond sounded nervous.

"I'm going to make the sky sharp."

"You're going to kill him." It wasn't a question.

"If he captures us, he won't just use our energy. He won't just kill us. He'll torture us. I can see it in his eyes. He wants us. Me. You. He wants our screams. I won't let him take us."

I reached out my hands and imagined that every falling flake was a sharp arrow. They slammed into our windshield, embedding inside the car. Their sharp tips a foot away from Redmond's face.

I looked up through the now gaping hole of the peeled roof to the Rider, but he fell far behind. He veered all over the road behind us. The arrows had gone into his helmet over and over again, right in the same spot, through his thick skin.

His bike went out of control and then fell, sliding across the road into the ditch. More and more ice arrows hit him. They hit his legs. His arms. Everywhere.

"There you go," I said to Redmond, who kept looking at me. "Ice can kill." Exhaustion took me over. For the first time ever, I let my guard down around someone. I felt his arm draw me close.

His heat protected me. Held me.

I fell asleep in his arms.

And I felt safe.
My new home was Redmond.

CHAPTER 26

Diary, Farrell is on my heels. I never thought I could hate someone so much. He does it on purpose. He lets me think I'm safe, that somehow, some way, he lost my scent and I can go back to a normal life. Normal for me, at any rate. But he comes again. He pops up, trying to scare me. Always with the same statement. "Gotcha. Nice smell."

I don't know what to do. Everything I've done, everything that's happened to me...I had something to do. Something to try. First, I escaped the facility and I just had to run. Now, though, running is pointless. He'll find me.

He always does. And I think he's let me run for so long because he doesn't really need me until I'm sixteen. But only a year left now. He won't let me go next time.

Right now, I'm in a library. Partly because I wanted some books to read, partly because there are people here. I'm protected for now. But when the library closes...This is all so useless.

Dammit! I see him. He's coming, Diary. He's talking to the librarians at the desk, charming them. He's pointing at me. They're...glaring at me? What is he telling them? I think they're calling the cops. I'm a runaway. Or a thief. Or I'm a murdering psycho. Who cares what he's telling them? I have to get out of here.

I won't freeze humans to get away.

~

I'm back. I can't believe what happened. I really can't. It's almost a miracle. I mean...Whoa. Sorry. Step by step. When I saw that Farrell was getting the help of the police, I had no choice. I jumped up. There was no need to hide my running. I barreled right through the glass. I knew it'd freeze and break on contact. I'm fairly sure that I'm more dangerous to the glass than it is to me. It explodes on impact with my extreme cold. Even when normal cold doesn't do a thing to glass, mine does.*

It's almost beautiful. I could see it in slow motion. The glass exploded and came down in showers.

Farrell was out the door right after me. I didn't expect him to wait. He's running out of time. The chase has to end.

I am used to running. I'm used to looking over my shoulder. So when I ran behind a building and onto another street, I wasn't looking at my feet. I fell.

I fell so long and so far, I thought I was in deep trouble. As I stayed there, my back hard against the ground, I thought it was over, Diary. I really did. I expected the hole up above me to show his face. Farrell laughing down at me, glad of my predicament.

I was bruised. The air was knocked out of me. I hit my head, so I couldn't see straight. Maybe I had a concussion. Good thing I heal fast. At least, I think I do. Another part of my being I don't have time to look into right now.

All in all, I was in no shape to fight or run. He had me.

But I waited. And waited. Almost sleeping but not quite.

And nothing happened!

Nothing! He missed me. He can't freaking smell me!

I am, like, to the moon. It's fantastic. I can breathe now. He can't freaking find me!

Yay! Yes! Hooray! Thank…well, whatever.

I'm going out in a few. I'm starving! I don't know why he lost my scent, but I'm free.

~

*N*ope. Not free. I just barely escaped him again. He came down on me while I was sneaking out of Wal-Mart. I pointed to the security cameras, and he glared, but I ran. I came back here. Oh, here is a sewer. You got it. A place where dreams go to die or something. It stinks. Not much. This access point hasn't been used in a long while. I don't know why. I'm not up to why cities decide to stop using certain access points.

I had fallen down an open manhole. I closed it. But Farrell is still not here. That means whatever is in this place stops him from finding my scent. I once read that dogs have trouble tracking through water. Well, there is a lot of old water around me. If that's the case, as long as some kind of water surrounds me, I'm safe. I could sleep in a swimming pool if I could stop the need for air. Oh, and stop it from freezing all around and losing the protection.

But I'll stay here. I mean, Diary! Don't judge it. What is a home but a place where you can feel safe? This is my home now. It's not great. I still have to sneak out and get food.

But Farrell can't find me in here.

I'll be back. My stomach is screaming at me. I gotta risk a run.

~

I hate Farrell! He doesn't know about this sewer access point. But he will. He's zeroing in on me. He's figuring out where it is I go to get off his radar. I can't take it. I won't take *it. If this is my new home, I have to do something to ensure I'll be safe. At least from other Breathers.*

Oh, you ask about Farrell, Diary? Oh, it's okay. Because I'm going to kill him.

CHAPTER 27

I think I died. I must have used up my powers and was in heaven.

As my eyes blinked into focus, I had trouble believing that what they were seeing was real. All around me was a quilted comforter with knitted shapes of mountains slipped in between each thread. The pillows were so soft they billowed up around my head.

Up above me were large wooden beams holding up a wooden roof. Two little tables next to my head held wonderfully warm lamps with round bulbs and forest green shades. Framed posters of mountains hung on the walls. And the bed, wow! It had four wooden posts with gigantic round knobs on them. A rocking chair was in the corner under a square window covered in mounds of curtains and lace.

Oh, and there was a person sitting in that chair.

"You're awake." She nodded toward me.

"Am I in heaven?" I asked.

"Some might think so. I certainly do. But as I am the proprietor of this establishment, I have my bias. This is not heaven, though. You're at my Bed and Breakfast. You feeling better?"

So, not heaven. I didn't answer. First, I had to figure out if she was friend or foe. And who she was. She was old, like forty. Her hair was braided, but it was a bright blonde. I looked into her eyes first. It had become a habit. No purple, relax; purple, get ready to fight.

Hers were deep brown—sun on a field kind of brown. She was wiry, tall, willowy. Her legs crossed like a grasshopper. I wondered if she was a model. She certainly looked the part.

"I am not a Breather," she said easily.

I hissed out an unexpected breath. "How…?"

She smiled. Her eyes were warm. "Let's just say your friend found his mountain."

I relaxed a little. "Where? Is it outside? Is it close? What do you know?"

"I am Natalie. I own the Mountain Lady Bed and Breakfast, where you are now. I'm guessing your friend figured out that the way to freedom is a bit obtuse."

I couldn't answer. Somehow, my brain couldn't put the facts together. We were here? There, I mean? The first clue to finding the fairy tale island. Redmond had figured it out. While I was asleep? I wasn't sure how to feel. I should be relieved, but I wasn't. It was too easy. Way too easy.

"Where's Redmond?" I asked. I flexed my fingers, feeling out for any energy I had.

Natalie brought a cup of coffee to her lips and sipped. She seemed unconcerned with my question. "In another room. He was almost as exhausted as you were. Dangerous stuff, attacking with the elements. It can drain you."

"Had no choice." I pushed the blankets off me and swung my legs out only to see they were covered in a soft nightgown. It felt so good against my skin. But I figured two things. One, I hadn't been wearing this before. Which meant, two, someone had undressed me.

"The nightgown was my doing. I hope you don't mind. Even with your skills, you can get sick if you wear the same clothing again and again. Not to mention the fact that they stunk to high heaven."

"Did Redmond see me naked?" I demanded. Funny that that was my first question. I should have been finding out how much Natalie knew and if she had a certain tendency to seek out Burners. She could have easily been a Breather. Instead, this was way more important to me. Great. After all my years on the run, I still turn into mush.

"Redmond is a gentleman. He left to change himself." Once again, she calmly sipped her coffee. It was starting to look really good, and I hated coffee.

"How do I know?" Now that I could stop internally blushing about Redmond seeing me in my altogether, I could get down to the important questions. Such as if Redmond was really alive and if I was in a Burner facility with no hope for escape. I had no idea, but I was betting on the doomed. My life didn't work like this. I didn't fall asleep and wake up halfway to my dream destination. "How do I know he's alive? How do I know you're not a Breather?"

She cocked her head and ran one fingertip down her cheek as if she were wiping away a tear. In its place an icy trail appeared, steam rising off it in the warm room. "Because I am a Burner, and I'd kill any Breather I met."

Something inside me froze, as if my own powers had finally taken my heart. I shook my head. I couldn't move for a few seconds. Natalie reminded me of all I left behind. Everyone. The ones even now reaching their deadly birthdays. I had run. Natalie didn't seem to be the same type.

"Wait," I said out loud. Anything to stop the inner ice storm. "You are drinking hot coffee."

Natalie laughed a little. "Still don't trust me? I don't blame you a bit. But my powers have faded over the years. I don't turn things as icy as I once did. Where did you come from anyway? Redmond told me he found out about his powers and went into hiding. He claims he doesn't know your story."

And he didn't. I hadn't told him much. "Where is the island?" I demanded. "If it's true that we've made it to the first part of the riddle, then where is *Freedom Boat*? Or is it even a boat at all?"

Natalie chuckled. "So, you found the tale. I started that rumor years ago. Oh, not to worry, it's quite true. I couldn't exactly tell the Breathers where it was or that it even existed, so I made it sound like a story complete with vague descriptions. I sent it along through my source inside the facilities. I had no idea Burners still believed in it. The boat is a submarine. But it takes a lot of doing. There hasn't been a run in a long time. I was starting to think there were no new Burners."

The ice moved up to my throat. There had been at least twenty children younger than me in the facility. Farrell must have been very good at his recruitment methods. Twenty teens now. About to be killed like Belinda. Natalie had no idea. I did. And I had thought *she* was the bad guy.

I stood up, ignoring how good the nightgown felt against my knees. How much I wanted to just stay in the comfortable bed where I almost felt human. "Where is it? And where are my clothes?"

"Sit. Relax."

Her tone was so strict that I had to listen. Well, I had to sit. I didn't have to relax.

"First, your clothes are in the fireplace. They were too small for your age. They stunk. And I don't even know what manner of liquids had frozen onto them. I sent someone out to get you new stuff. Some special stuff. It will help a bit to regulate your body. You can eat and drink normally in them."

I gaped. Like what Farrell had given me. And I thought I had outgrown them. "How?"

"There are certain materials that suppress what we are." She crossed her legs and sat back. Once again coffee disappeared down her throat. "Once you get new clothes, I will arrange with another source for the submarine to come around. You will get on it. You will be free."

Free…Like Belinda had claimed. Free…Unlike everyone else who would just die. "But the Breathers can find us! How long before they track you down?"

She set her cup down and stood up. In seconds she was next to me. And the strange lady was hugging me. Me! It wasn't like Redmond. I hadn't had an adult's affection ever. And this woman I had just met was giving me comfort.

I surprised myself and fell onto her shoulder. She clutched me tight. "I know," she murmured. "It's been a hard life. You've been hunted at every turn. You don't know who to trust. But whenever you have this much pain, the powers that be have to give equal joy. It's the law."

Stupid icy tears rolled down my cheeks. "How is it the law?"

"It just is." She held the back of my head tightly.

I don't know how long I held her. But I didn't let go. I was hugging my mom. I was hugging my dad. I was hugging the fake persona of who they were. Finally, it dawned on me. I was hugging a strange Burner!

I pulled away, and she let me. "Uh, thanks. It must work for all of us, huh?"

She returned to her coffee but shot me a questioning look. "What?"

"The allure." I pulled the blankets back over me, snuggling into the comfort. If Natalie was right, I had nothing to worry about here. If she was wrong, I didn't want to run in this soft nightgown. I'd have to wait until the new promised clothes showed up. "When I met Redmond, I practically fainted from his beauty. And now I think of you as a motherly figure. All part of that allure."

Natalie laughed. "Whoever told you about yourself didn't tell you enough. To others you are a goddess descending from the heavens to earth. But to other Burners, you are normal. We are immune to each other's powers just like the ice. If you had hugged a mortal with as much ferocity, they would have become ice statues. The same is true about the allure. I like you, kid. Because you remind me of me. I once was where you are. I was hunted. I thought I'd never reach twenty. I hated everyone. And I felt sorry for you. So, I hugged you. But if you think I was drawn forth by our mystical abilities..." She shook her head. "Nope. Doesn't work like that."

Again, this information sent shivers inside. If Redmond wasn't affected by any allure...If I wasn't...

"Wow," Natalie said and held her hand over her mouth. "I didn't think something like that would freak you out more than the Breathers on your tail."

I quickly controlled my face. Natalie had seen too much. "When are my clothes getting here? I can't stay."

"You'll have them before you know it. But this place is safe. It's off the Breathers' radar. It's complicated. But the location is the important thing. You ever heard that dogs have trouble tracking a scent through water? Well, when you're surrounded by it, Burners are the same." She stood up and drew my curtains. I gasped. The ocean was right outside my window. I should have known. I cursed my lack of observance. I should have noted that the underlying roar I could hear meant the ocean was nearby.

"That's why the island is safe. Breathers hate water. They won't find you where so much of it roars with nature's ferocity."

Somehow, I was calmed by the repeated movement of the waves. The sun was up, glinting sparkles against the blue. All I saw was the expanse of water. My frozen insides melted a little. We were almost there.

"Why don't I leave you to rest? Your clothing will be delivered. When it is, you can check out my Bed and Breakfast. You can eat in here or down in the dining room. There are all sorts of activities. Tennis. There's an indoor pool." She stood up and made her way to the exit.

"Pool?" I asked. "Are you insane?"

"Oh, it's heated."

I wondered if she was crazy.

Natalie grinned at my expression. "In the past, this was my favorite part. To meet a Burner so sure of everything. I told you the clothing I'll give you would help. There will be a swimsuit too."

I wondered if any of this was possible. I had fallen asleep in hell and awoken in heaven. Did I deserve to end up in heaven? Everything was being solved around me. I might be able to swim? I'd be able to eat and drink normally?

And Redmond actually *liked* me for me, not some allure?

I swirled the blankets over my head and breathed in the smell of fresh linens. I closed my eyes and just enjoyed myself. I would do that, I declared. It didn't matter about anyone else. It only mattered about me. Hadn't I suffered enough? Hadn't I earned the right to be comfortable?

I fell asleep, not worrying about what was after me for the first time.

～

*T*he clothing Natalie promised was brought to me. It was left outside my room in a little box. She knocked once and then left. I felt the fabric, expecting the same thick, rubbery stuff from the facility. Instead, my fingers met softness. It was shimmery colorful material. But there was something different about it. I didn't know where it came from or what made it so, but as soon as I put it all on, I felt…new.

But there were no more excuses to stay in bed. And Redmond was flashing through my mind. I wanted to see him more than I wanted breakfast. My stomach didn't agree. It gurgled and growled about how long it had been since I'd last fed it. My heart got her way, though.

The hallway outside my room was a long wooden thing. Thick logs had been hewn out to make walls and ceilings. Runner carpets stretched against each other, meeting with matching patterns. Rows of doors ran alongside mine, but the other wall was filled with windows that looked out into a forest.

I had no idea where Redmond was. I jumped as another guest left her room. "Oh, excuse me," she said, but then she stopped and stared. I tried to ignore her as she walked down the hall. She was normal. Normal. Not like me. I was around normal people!

I stood there like a statue until another voice said behind me, "Excuse me." Another guest. Another normal person. I moved aside but not enough, and he brushed me in passing. I expected him to yelp with pain, but he just kept going. He hadn't seen me, so he didn't stare.

I hadn't hurt him. I hadn't burned him. These clothes…I felt my face crumpling. I hadn't felt this free since I was in the facility, before Belinda…It was all coming back. Who I had left behind. What would happen to them.

"Hey!"

Redmond.

I turned to see him walking up to me with a great big grin on his face. I would have earlier attributed it to my allure. Now…The boy was in love with me. Hell, yeah!

He, too, wore what I did. His powers were reined in. Controlled. Two Burners who were no longer wild. I probably shouldn't have been so obsessed with a shirt. But I really liked his sweater. It was a blue button-up. It curved around his well-defined lines. His shaggy blonde hair touched his shoulders with disregard. And his pants. Oops, better not look down there.

"Hi." I sounded shy. Crap. "Redmond."

"Laoni. You look absolutely, insanely beautiful. Clean clothes agree with you."

Zing. Better do it back. "And non-burned ones look awesome on you." *I want to touch your clothes.* I didn't add that, thank goodness. I felt contained, my powers in place, but my thoughts were wilder than ever before. Bucking like a bronco. Redmond liked me for me!

"Red," I said slowly. "Can I call you Red?"

He wrinkled his nose. We both shifted our weight at the same time. The outside light played across Redmond's face, moving like wind through leaves. "It's a little obvious. Long name, shorten, nickname, check. Hate that."

"Okay, Mond. How about that? It's moon in German."

He laughed. "How do you know these things?"

The facility let us learn, I silently answered him. *And I loved languages.* "I just do," I said out loud.

"Well, that sounds cool. Okay, call me Mond."

"Mond, I was wrong." I had to be honest. I didn't know where I was going. I just wanted to say his name. My thoughts weren't letting me in on where they'd end up. Once again, I shifted. "We are immune to each other's allure. I really do like you."

Yep. My mouth betrayed me again. I'd wanted to keep that secret. My idiot brain…

Mond didn't mind. "That's what I was telling you!"

My mouth gaped. "How! When? You believed me, remember?"

"Nope."

"Yep."

He grinned again and reached forward to grab a strand of my hair. He wound it gently around his finger. The stark white against his dusky fingers made for a great contrast. "So, now we know, and we're safe. Natalie told you, right?"

I shook my head. "She *said* we were safe. But there—" I shut up as more guests walked past, giving us wondering stares before moving toward the carpeted staircase that led down. "Normal people. We can't be safe here. Even with water surrounding us."

Mond stole my hand. I didn't want it back. He reached his fingers up to the inner side of my wrist and gave me a tug. "We're safe. The moment I came near the water I felt… better. No one has come close. And you have to admit, ever since we left the sewer we've been attacked. Out of the blue, *bam.*"

He pulled me to the staircase. I had no idea where we were going. I didn't care.

"But no one. In the last twelve hours, not a breath of a Breather."

"Okay." I believed him. I believed Natalie. Mostly, I believed in how much I wanted this to be a normal day. Plus, if we were safe, I could really start to get interested in what Mond and I could do together. "So…what will we do?"

"I want to date."

My heart fell. "You met someone here so fast?"

Mond stopped on the stairs, still holding my hand. I was above him. His face looked more ruggedly handsome than ever before, his wild hair falling to his back. "No, silly. I want to date you."

Right. I should have known that. "We can't date."

"Why not?"

"Because, um, danger. Death. Secret fairy tale island that we need to find."

"All on the backburner, if you'll forgive the fitting expression."

I laughed. Crap. I was laughing easily. I had to be more careful.

"I'm thinking breakfast. Did Natalie tell you about these clothes?"

I nodded. "Normal food. Normal water."

"Orange juice!" he said enthusiastically. "Un-evaporated orange juice. Non-burnt toast. White eggs instead of charcoal."

I was getting into the spirit of things. "Orange juice not from concentrate!"

"Um, just frozen orange juice," he pointed out. "Concentrate would be, you know, condensed."

I slapped his shoulder as we continued down. "I was just using hyperbole."

"Hyper what now?"

"For someone so smart, you can be dumb."

"I'm smart where it counts, unlike some ice girls," he teased back.

I think I was blushing. There was a hidden declaration in his words. "Then, after a wonderfully unburnt and unfrozen breakfast, what?"

"A walk on the beach."

"Then tennis," I said. All my worries were falling away. Mond was right. This place was safe.

"Swimming!" he said.

I nodded. "Yes! Surfing!"

"Whoa!" he said. We had reached a bigger area that opened to a ground floor that stretched in both directions. A dining room was through one alcove, and through another I saw the wooden front desk. Large windows revealed trees on one side and the ocean on the other. Beyond the large glass doors, I saw a larger wooden building neighboring this one. It must have held the tennis court and the pool. On the other side I saw stables.

"Even if it wasn't way too cold, surfing is too athletic for me. It's dangerous."

I giggled at his expression. I moved in on his personal space as he leaned against the wall. "Don't tell me the fire controller is afraid of drowning."

"Maybe a little. But I'm more afraid of sharks. The ocean isn't a tame beast."

I nodded. "Okay. I was just, I don't know…"

"Feeling free. Feeling like you could do anything?"

I nodded. He got it. Because he was the same. "Besides, who knows how long before the submarine can come. We better do the best stuff."

Mond nodded. I finished taking his space and leaned against his chest. I breathed in his new clothes, still tinged with smoke, and the underlying scent that was just him. I was getting too used to his scent. He leaned his chin on my head.

"What's happening?" he asked in a whisper.

"First love," I responded. I was only being partly ironic. It wasn't only first love, it was last love. Only love. True love.

A guest cleared his throat and we got out of his way— keeping our faces turned away—and headed to a table that showed the ocean. Mond grabbed a menu and started saying things like, "Yes, I'll take that, and that, and that. Ooh, not burned! That!"

I did the same. We had ordered nearly the whole menu as Natalie walked up to us. We were too busy feeding our faces to notice her walking across the dining room. There were only a few guests eating breakfast, but they were across the room. I had had no idea how good food could taste. I kept eating even when my stomach was full. I loved these clothes!

"Good to see you two up and happy," Natalie said. "The *Freedom* will be docking tomorrow, okay?"

I patted the seat next to me for her to sit down. She was already my friend. Already someone I'd have to leave behind again. "So soon? And here?"

Natalie shook her braid, letting it whip against her cheek a bit. "No, not here. Gotta keep this place off their radar."

Their. The Breathers. The safety of this place was tarnished a bit. "Yeah. Good idea."

"Couldn't we just stay here?" Mond asked, keeping his hand over his mouth as he finished his bites. "I mean, we're safe. Water. A nice Bed and Breakfast next to the ocean. A great ally who's like us."

Oh, I guess she'd also told Mond what she was.

"I can think of worse places to live out our lives."

Natalie's eyes darkened. There was pain in there. "No." She reached out and took Mond's hand to lessen her harshness. "Not because I wouldn't love you here. You two know all too well what it's like to have no one similar around. One Burner isn't obvious. Three together for a short time isn't either. But when Burners come together, people start to notice."

"How?" I asked. I too would have liked to stop running. I knew nothing about this island. I knew I liked it here so far. And I liked Natalie. The mother I wanted.

Natalie leaned on her fingers, but her first one pointed

obscurely to the others in the dining room. Ah. I got it. They were all staring at us now. Every single one of them. By myself, I got a quick look. Together, Mond and I had gotten more attention. But now, everyone was openly staring at us. They had forgotten their meals, taken in by the impossible beauty of three gods in their midst.

"I'd better get back to work," Natalie said and stood up. "The details will be in your rooms tonight. I don't dare speak here. Be ready to travel at five in the morning."

Of course. More running. I couldn't stay here. I couldn't stay anywhere.

"The island," Mond reminded, reading my mind. "We'll find a home there. In the meantime, let's just get away from people."

I leaned back in my chair. I didn't want anything more from the multiple plates in front of me. Already the richness of what I just wasn't used to swirled my stomach into an unhappy tornado. "How? This is a crowded Bed and Breakfast. They'll probably want the pool. The beach. The tennis court."

"Not if we hurry. The earlier we go, the earlier we get the worm."

I glared at him. "I don't want the worm. I want the pool."

He laughed and jumped up.

"You've changed," I noted. "You're becoming annoyingly cheery."

He wiggled his eyebrows. "Things are getting better. You ever notice that when things are bad, they just keep getting worse?"

I nodded.

"Well, it's opposite now. We've eaten a real breakfast. We're going to swim without evaporating the water or freezing it. We are together now. Fully. I don't know. I see life as getting better. I'd better get that half-empty glass back, because it's overflowing."

I had to agree. How could either of us stay down for long? Ever since Redmond appeared, I felt happier and happier. Now, it was almost impossible for me to fight his optimism. What a change! Especially since he was a pessimist before he met me. Being with me had changed him. And the same was true for the opposite.

"I'm letting go now," I responded. "I'm relaxing."

"Me, too!"

He took my hand, and we took the two glass doors outside. They led onto a deck which had wooden stairs all the way down to the beach. I heard our feet clunking against each beam. A light breeze tickled my face. It was cold. Wow. Cold. Never felt that before. The clothing was doing more than just letting us eat normally. I felt the temperature. It wasn't bad at all…The sun was spilling its light across the waves, caressing the shore.

As Mond moved his fingers over the back of my hand, I ignored what had just made me depressed. How could I stay sad long? The first guy I loved loved me back. I couldn't even say that about the first people I loved. My parents hadn't loved me. Despite the cold, we both pulled our shoes off and walked through the sand, letting it spill between our toes.

"What was it like?" I asked.

Mond looked at me quizzically. "Huh?"

"Having parents. Did your dad love you?"

He swung my arm as he reached down to pick up a shell. He looked at all its intricacies before he answered. "I think he did. He didn't show it. He was raised to keep emotions hidden. Love was a weakness. He took every opportunity to remind me of my failures just so he wouldn't love me. He was the same with Mom. That's why she left. He blamed me.

But…I'm starting to realize it was his own fault. Things have changed for me, Oni."

Oh, he was doing the same thing I was. I wouldn't tell him that oni was a demon in Japanese folklore. I couldn't.

"I tried to fight my feelings for you, just like he did Mom. I followed his example. But then I hated that example. And I let go. I should have told him."

"Told him what?"

"Keeping emotions in can only lead to pain. It was why he turned to the bottle. It was the only way to let it out. A security blanket when all he needed was to talk. How much better could it have been if he had just used words and not bottles? He'd still be alive. Those people would still be alive. I think anyway. Maybe I would have exploded anyway."

"No, I don't believe that."

"How come?"

I moved closer to him until our shoulders touched. I wanted contact. Now that I knew all this was real, it terrified me. But it was better than a fairy tale. And I just needed him now more than ever.

"Because you're not angry. If anyone would explode, I would. Your powers came out of fear. If…" I shut up. There was no reason to talk more about this. "Hey, tidepools! I'll bet we'll find some cool looking stuff."

Mond laughed. "Yep, the ocean is full of cool stuff."

"Don't mock me, you," I said.

The wind picked up and moved his hair like the waves. Warmth filled me and I squeezed his hand harder. "We're real, right?"

"Real as the ocean."

"And as dangerous," I couldn't help retorting.

Mond smiled. That's all. Smiling at this new danger. "Most things worthwhile are dangerous."

Ah, he had me. That was it. My common sense was gone.

I had been under direct threat for the last four years and dangerous my whole life. But everything fell away. Everything became walking on the beach with Mond. I could even ignore the looks everyone gave us as we walked.

We walked and talked. Mond mainly about his past. Me mainly about our present. The near future was forgotten, and I already had ignored my past. After we checked out the tidepools, we went and played tennis. I never had before. Mond hadn't either, so we spent the time running back and forth just trying to actually hit the ball.

But then the other court took on two guests, and the looks they gave us reminded me why we had to keep hidden. That was no fun. We quickly went onto swimming. Now, that was deserted. Even though it was heated and indoors, people felt the effects of the season. Instinctively, they stayed away from the pool.

Which meant we had it all to ourselves. And as Mond stepped out of the changing area and I saw his wonderful legs and his perfect torso, I was too glad we were alone. I had never been privileged to so much of his skin before. His shorts were by no means tight, but I couldn't catch my breath at his shoulders. His knees. His feet. All unclothed. All lines and muscles exposed.

His eyes also couldn't quite focus on my face. I had been bold. I wore a two piece. Red. It caught and held his eyes. "I wear a bikini well, too, don't I?" I asked.

He couldn't answer. There was a light in his eyes. Like he was under some kind of trance.

"Hey! I thought you were immune to the allure!" I complained.

"This has nothing…Nothing to do with that and everything to do with the fact that I don't think good now."

"Huh?" I felt a smile touching my cheeks. This was too good! I had been locked away from others for so long, I had never felt normal. And neither had Mond. No, this wasn't my allure. This was good old-fashioned boy and girl interaction.

I snapped my fingers. "Come on, now. We have to focus. Swimming, remember?" I jumped in. Never learned how to dive. Wish I had. I would have liked to feel Mond's appreciation for a graceful form. I surfaced again.

"So that's what it feels like!" I screamed. I didn't know how to control the level of my voice. I was too excited. "It's warm!"

Mond jumped in himself, and I saw my own euphoria spread across his face. "Wow! I'm immersed in water again!"

"It's all around me. Water! Hey, I have no weight!" I kicked my legs. I didn't know how to swim. Somehow that fact eluded me. I suddenly didn't know how to move through the water.

"How do I move?"

Mond caught on immediately and was next to me in seconds. Suddenly all his skin was close up. Extremely close up. He held his arms under mine. It felt different. Not the same as it was without the swimsuits. "Never learned how to swim?"

"Had ice too early." I swallowed. I was weightless. But it had nothing to do with the water. "You?"

"Every year since I turned five, my dad took me to the community pool."

"Lucky," I said.

"Yeah. I guess so." But again his meaning changed. His hand under the water moved to clutch my back. His other reached down to smooth against my legs. "Just use these to kick. Keep above water. Remember never to panic. And we should stay in the shallow end." He towed me forth. Now my feet could touch bottom.

"I have to remember all my lessons. After a while, you just do it by habit and forget learning."

I had other questions. "Mond, have you ever done other stuff?" I swished closer in the water, pressing my belly against his. I found our skins' connection absolutely fascinating.

"Other stuff?"

"This is new for me. I've been on the run even when I hit puberty. I had to figure out stuff on my own. But you lived normally."

He swallowed. I didn't know how. But I wanted to get closer. I pressed so hard against him I could see no line. "Laoni," he said, but he couldn't keep a grunt out of his voice. "I never have…I mean, my first girlfriend I gave a burn to by hugging her. I burnt her lips. I never even tried. Somehow I knew…"

I felt his heart under his skin. "So, you've never…"

"Never."

"Not yet."

I reached up to connect further. His hands grabbed around my waist as I took his lips in mine. I explored his muscles with my hands, lowering until I settled on his backside. He also gripped me. "Laoni," he whispered. I could hear the excitement in his voice.

"Not here," I whispered. I broke away from his touch. My throat was too tight. But a life on the run couldn't make me forget completely about people. Any minute now someone could fight back against the season and walk in. And I certainly didn't like them staring at me when I was fully clothed.

"But now?" he asked.

My stomach tightened. "Always now. Tomorrow we're running again. We may never reach the island. I've eaten. I've swam. But I haven't…"

"Let's go!" He needed no more conversation.

But I had some ground rules. We both showered first—I wanted to be clean from the smelly chlorine in the pool. And I wanted to head back to my room and wait for him. I wanted him to knock on my door.

So about thirty minutes later, I was sitting on my bed, and I heard his knock. As I let him in, I noticed his hair was still wet from the shower. I closed the door behind him and brought his wet hair to my face. I rubbed against all the droplets of water. I still liked the tickle on my skin. He just grunted under my touch.

I let his head come up, but it didn't stay for long. He covered my mouth with his.

I knew what I wanted. This was the one and only chance. I knew this was a heaven we wouldn't get again.

There it was. I didn't believe in Belinda's fairy tale. I had gotten Mond believing, but I never had. I just had wanted to believe to make Mond happy. He would never have stayed in that sewer. He would have left me.

Mond's strong fingers took my buttons in his hands. I was very glad I had decided to dress again.

I had no idea how fun it'd be to undress. The sensations changed as we lost our clothing that tamed us.

We turned wild.

CHAPTER 28

*D*ear Diary,

I am alone. I will always be alone. I left behind every single person who ever meant anything to me. The Breathers are dead that chased me. They won't find me in my new home. I live.

Oh, who the hell am I kidding? This isn't living! I scurry out and steal food I can barely taste. It's been almost a year since I found this place. No Breathers. But I'm not happy. I hate it here. It stinks more and more every day. There's only one real area I can stay in. I miss everyone. It's almost good to run. You don't get the chance to think.

I have to steal everything I get. And Farrell's death scream still rings in my mind. The only one I feel guilty for. Ugh, Farrell. Just thinking about that creep makes me angry.

You know, Diary, I won't lie here. I thought of Farrell as my father. He wasn't. Or maybe he was. My real father betrayed me, but so did Farrell. I thought he loved me. I thought he loved all of us. But he showed his real face.

Still, my home is gone. My friends are gone. My family is gone. Dammit. If I had normal tears, this diary would be soaked. But no. *My icy tears run down my cheeks and make stupid plopping noises in the water. I am ice. I wish my heart were.*

No, Diary. I have to make it ice. My emotions lie to me. I thought my father loved me. Nope! He sold me out. I thought Mom loved me. Try again! She hated me when I accidentally hurt her. I thought of the facility as my home. Wrong again! Thanks for playing! It was my prison.

Now, here I am, wearing clothes too small, I'm filthy, and I've just stolen food from the supermarket. Luckily, I got some Cheetos. They work well in my stomach. I wonder if it's the salt in them.

Diary, I can't stay here. Not for the rest of my life. Maybe I could still go and look for Belinda's island.

Either that or die trying.

Right, honesty. Die trying is what I'm expecting.

CHAPTER 29

A knock on the door woke me. Mond's head was on my shoulder. I felt warm all over, even though I actually couldn't be. It wasn't like I was wearing anything. This warmth came from inside. I had never known how good it could feel to be with someone that way.

"Mond," I whispered. "I think Natalie is here with our instructions for tomorrow."

He muttered but didn't move. I guess he was worn out.

"Come on. We need to get dressed."

"No." He wasn't getting up.

I shook my head. I had no embarrassment. Living on your own, you make your own rules. And I had broken none. Let Natalie see Mond under all my blankets. I slipped on my shirt and pants and went to open the door.

Sure enough, Natalie stood there. She saw Mond in a heartbeat but didn't even blink. She did raise one eyebrow about the singed blankets. There were black holes from where Mond had gotten a little…overheated. But she said nothing about that. She just slammed the door and stood in front of me with her arms crossed in front of her. "Good, you're together. Redmond, wake up. Now."

His eyes flashed open. I guess he didn't expect her to summon him. He sat up, letting the blanket fall to his waist. I was a bit distracted by his skin.

"Focus!" Natalie scolded me. "If you make it to the island, there will be plenty of time for this later." She sounded sharper than normal.

"What is it? Are you angry that we…" I gestured to the bed.

Natalie laughed with a short bark. "The blankets are easy to replace. And as far as you two doing stuff together… Well, I'm not much for morals. I know we get what we can when we can or else we don't get it at all. No, I'm not here to lecture you on morality. We've got problems."

Mond slipped on his shirt and quickly dressed the rest of the way while Natalie turned her head away.

"What is it?" I asked. Back to business. Fallen down from heaven.

"The submarine is early."

"What?" I asked.

"You have to hurry and go. About a mile down the beach there's a dock. Right next to that dock, the submarine will rise."

I held up my hand. "Wait, why? Why so early?"

Natalie bit her lip. "I don't know. They didn't tell me. All I can figure is that someone intercepted the message for tomorrow, so they have to come sooner. Doesn't matter. If you don't move now, you could be tracked here. And I don't want that."

"Because you're safe here, right?" Mond asked. I heard the fire in his voice.

Natalie hissed. "No, because *every* Burner who comes through here is safe. Everyone who wants a safe future, who wants to get to the island. I have sent quite a few that way. And I won't risk the future of this operation by having Breathers figure us out. Secrecy! That's what I need."

I growled. "If they intercepted your message, how secret is this place?"

Natalie sighed. "The communication is faulty. It goes through multiple channels. There's a facility nearby that I'm in contact with, and email is not exactly the most secure thing."

I froze. A facility nearby? What did that mean? "Natalie," I said slowly. "Are there…Burners there?"

Mond shot me a look, but I couldn't return his gaze.

Natalie sighed. "I guess you should know. They recently moved the New York facility here."

We shared a look. I knew what she wasn't saying. She knew there were Burners there, but she couldn't save them. She wouldn't dare. It was way too dangerous.

"Where?" I asked, not really knowing why.

"About twenty miles east of here." Natalie was staring at me with suspicion. "It's much too fortified."

I snorted. Like I'd ever put myself in harm's way to save anyone.

"The point here is that you need to move now. My allies could have been compromised. Just, please, get to safety. Where you are now isn't real. It's an illusion."

She shoved envelopes into our hands. "My letter of introduction. Give it to a woman named Nora on the submarine. She will take care of you. Don't worry, you'll know who she is." And with that, Natalie spun around and left. She didn't say goodbye. She didn't even look at us.

There was nothing for it. We both finished getting dressed, grabbed what little there was of our stuff, and left the hotel.

We walked along the beach again. But this time, it wasn't

for fun. It wasn't even that enjoyable. The sun was already gone behind the gray sheet of clouds and it was getting darker. I would have much more preferred it getting lighter. I would have been happier had it been five in the morning. Instead, it was stretching toward evening.

"So, here we are." Mond's tone sounded light. He wanted to hold my hand again. I kept it away. Didn't he understand? That was only for heaven. "On our way to freedom." His tone had darkened a bit when I pulled my hand away. He didn't get it. He may have been hiding for years, but not on the run.

"Yeah."

"Okay, what? It's just happening sooner than we thought. Who cares if it's tonight or tomorrow? The point is we're on our way."

"Mond." I felt tears starting. Oh, real tears. Not the ice drops. Water was running down my face. Now, that tickle I did *not* like. "We're on the run again. I liked that place. I liked Natalie."

"Yeah, but there will be new places, new people."

I tried to make him understand. "We don't have any proof of that. No truth about where our lives will end up. Any minute now, a Breather could pop out and we'll have to kill or be killed. It gets old. And that place just felt like home." I couldn't control myself. "I've had three homes in my life. My parents' home, the facility, and Natalie's Mountain Lady, no matter how briefly. And all are gone. And all the people who were my family are gone too."

Mond didn't answer for a few minutes as our feet hit the sand in unison. We were far enough away from the waves that they didn't lap toward us. But their quiet sound didn't soothe me anymore. The roar invaded my head.

"All the people?" Mond finally asked.

Oops.

"Umm, yeah."

"What people? I thought you were captured and imprisoned in some insane facility. You liked *them?*"

I shook my head. I didn't want Mond to know about Cindy and Erin. Not about the many cooks and staff that I assumed had loved me. "I was fooled."

"You thought of it as home." Mond was working through something in his head. "And you had brothers and sisters."

He caught me off guard, which was why I just answered him, "Yes."

"Other Burners were there." It all settled on him. I didn't like his face at that moment. It was still as handsome as ever, and, to my surprise, I still felt a good sort of ache in my heart when I looked at him. But his disapproval was clear.

My world was ending. Right here and right now.

"Yes. I left them. I abandoned them. I got away so quick it would make your head spin. I had that dust coming up from my feet like you see in cartoons. I was *whoosh!* Out of there." Acid poured from my voice. I spilled it onto Mond. My moon.

"So, where are they? Dead? What happens when they catch us?"

"Not yet. They're not sixteen yet. They're in that new facility. We've got a whole lot of energy in our bodies. Belinda, my best friend, was killed. Now, I know she was drained. The others were younger than me, so not old enough, but soon will be. Dead, dead, dead. Yep. I'm a monster."

"Old enough?" Mond stopped, pulling me on the arm. Strange, his touch still felt gentle. "What does that mean?"

"I guess as a source of power, we have to get strong enough. At a young age, we are too explosive. At an old age, we're too weak. But just after we turn sixteen, we're usually just right."

Mond's fingers stroked up to my shoulder and pulled me into a hug. "What you've been through," he murmured into my hair. "I get it. I know you had to do what you had to do."

No! He was *not* forgiving me for this. "I didn't. I could have saved them all. In less than a year, the ones I knew will all be dead. Then in a few more years, the rest. All while I'm on my way to freedom! Hurray for me. Too bad, so sad for the rest."

Mond pulled away and put a gentle kiss on my forehead. "No way. Because we're going to save them all."

I wasn't sure I heard what I thought I did. "Umm, freedom is that way," I said, pointing down the darkening beach. The endless horizon turned even more so as black hit darker black.

"Not for them. Not for our kind. Laoni, I never knew how many there were of us. I always felt alone. When you told me about the island, I didn't believe in it. The truth is, I hadn't seen much yet. But after all the stuff that happened, after meeting you, I've realized that there is something to hope for."

"Me? I'm a runner. I saved myself. I've killed. I've lived like a roach, scurrying around as the years marched forward for the ones I left behind. I'm not anything to hope for."

Somehow, his lips found mine and I got caught up again —feeling the surge of power that had brought me so much joy before. "Don't be down on yourself or I'll do it again," he said.

"I'm a monster," I said, but I expected the next kiss. I melted, metaphorically, right into his arms.

"We can save them. I'm not done with that Ferrari. I'm not ready for a submarine. It's a little too confined. Besides, I would like some company."

I held my hands around his waist and laid my head on his chest as I thought about what he was saying. What it meant.

Going back. Running, but toward danger. All to save the only family I had ever known.

"Breathers will be there. All three kinds."

"Yeah, so will flammable stuff. And water in the pipes. I say we lay siege."

I laughed, though I felt like eating barbed wire. "Redmond," I scolded, using his full name on purpose. "You have to understand what this might mean. We might die too. No freedom. No island. No seventeenth birthday."

"Nah. It means safety, freedom, just a bit later and with a lot more friends."

I had no smile on my face now. I couldn't even understand why my feet were turned around and heading back to the Mountain Lady's parking lot. "It won't be easy. When I was there, Breathers came and went from that place all the time. You've seen…"

I trailed off as Mond gave me a look. "Laoni, my life hasn't been easy. I'm used to it. And, really, save your breath if anything is coming that tries to talk me out of this. It's the right thing to do. My dad never did the right thing. I won't follow in his footsteps. There are others out there. Burners. People like us. Like me. Like you. People who will have a very hard life as soon as they reach the age that's supposed to be the start of life, not the end."

I scoffed. "You only want a second choice for a girlfriend."

Mond once again stopped me. Before I knew it, he swept me off my feet and held me in my arms. "Laoni, you're stubborn. Angry. You have an unhealthy love of Cheetos. You scare me sometimes with your intensity."

"Yeah, I'm a ball of stupid, right?"

I didn't even have time to blink before he was kissing me —his lips pressed hard into mine. "No insults, remember?"

I nodded. I wanted to insult myself all evening if it meant

more of his insanely powerful kisses. But I knew our plans didn't include that.

"I was just pointing out that I didn't fall for you because I can kiss you. I kiss you because I fell for you. I'm way out of my element for how I feel about you. If you said let's go on, I'd forget the other Burners."

I blinked. I shifted my weight in his arms, so I could feel his fingers stronger on my hip. "You would?"

"Yes."

"But you feel so strongly…"

"When a boy loves a girl, there is nothing else to feel strongly about. It's you, Laoni. Everything is you. The world is smaller if you're not in it. My fire would dim if I couldn't hold you."

I swallowed and pushed my head into his neck. "Then, let's save them."

I looked up into his eyes. We stared at each too long, but finally, he let me down and we walked again. We didn't tell Natalie for two reasons. One, I didn't want her coming with us. She may have had some ice powers, but like she said, her operation here was much more important. And two, because we wanted to be alone up to the siege.

Though it wouldn't be a siege. We discussed our plans as Mond drove toward the facility. The Ferrari's roof had been fixed, melted back together by Mond's fire. He had been busy as I slept. I could see a seam in the roof, but that was it.

It was obvious, at least to me, where the facility was located. It looked the same as the one I had escaped from. Bordered by forest, hidden by leaves. I could find my way inside in my sleep. I knew its path. The road was bordered by forest, and soon enough, it was blocked by a huge gate and miles of electrified fence.

There it was. The facility. Home.

CHAPTER 30

*D*ear Diary,

    Belinda and I are forming our own club. Cindy is invited because I can't get her off my tail. And Erin is too, but she bugs me. I hope we can get rid of her.

Our club's name?

Super Secret Spies.

Our purpose?

To survey. Well, I'd like to say it's to spy, because that's the name of our club. But it's more important, or so Belinda says, to get a hold of our surroundings. So, we sneak around the building. We don't have much security around here. No one really watches us. They let us play all day long. They only care about when we go to bed and get up in the morning.

Erin snuck off yesterday. She came back to tell us there were only two security doors—one on the way out to the parking lot and the other to our play yard.

We all separated today. I went to the south side. It was so much fun. Everyone I saw patted me on the head, and then they walked on. It doesn't feel so secret when everyone knows. I have to get better.

~

Diary,

I've gotten better. I managed to sneak around Farrell. I followed him for a full hour and he didn't sense me. I have checked the perimeter. I reported back to Belinda and she gave me a big smile and a "Good girl." Her simple words make me much happier than any pats on the heads from the adults.

I think Belinda is sneaking around tonight. She seems so serious. As I sit here on the corner of my bunk bed, I'm actually starting to wonder. Does Belinda think of this as a game anymore?

But of course, we're spies. Spies lead dangerous lives. I better take this seriously too. I need a hat and a trench coat. You always see spies wearing hats and trench coats.

I will be better. I want to make Belinda happy. She'll see.

~

Diary,

Belinda yelled at me. I had to write. It's like midnight now. She was so mean. I caught her coming back. I asked how it went. She didn't answer and just climbed onto the bunk above me. I put my head up there to talk to her and she told me to leave her alone.

Mean, that's what she is. I just wanted to know what she had found out. She said that she was going to look at the computers. But did she? And if she did, what did she find out?

Or did she even find anything out? Maybe she's just being mean. Well, I don't care! I was just asking what she had done and she bit my head off. I won't talk to her again. I hate her.

Still...I wonder. What did she find out?

CHAPTER 31

We weren't stupid enough to drive the car right to the enemy's gates. As soon as I saw the familiar setup, I told Redmond to drive off the road. There was a little gap between the trees, so we just sat there, old trees staring down at the somewhat mangled Ferrari, though patched up a bit.

"Should we scout it out first?" Redmond asked. Once again, he was turning toward me. I was the leader here. The one with a lot more experience.

But I had never been the attacker. I mean, once, with Farrell, when I drew him to me, but I hadn't attacked him. I had waited. The silence in the car after his question deafened me. He wanted me to tell him what to do.

"Redmond, I…" But I couldn't say I didn't know what to do. And information would be good. "How stealthy are you?" I asked.

He gave me a grin. "I'm good. Really good."

"Then go. Skirt the perimeter and tell me if you see a good way in. No front doors, okay?"

He gave me a pout. "Aww, and I wanted to run in there fire burning."

I fought a grin. He made me smile even when we were discussing certain death scenarios. "Go. Please."

"Yes, my captain!"

He quietly opened the door. I could hear the crunch of rocks and dirt and leaves under his feet as he snuck away, but soon enough, I heard nothing. He was quiet. I was a ball of nerves. Since we met each other, we had been together. Not separated. And here we were, readying for battle.

How could it feel so right? My whole time on the run, I was saving myself. That should have felt right. But here and now, I was heading back for probably the certain death of me and Redmond, but I was…happy. I was doing what I needed to do to make up for everything I had done.

I was finally fulfilling Belinda's request.

And it felt awesome!

I jumped a mile when a face came up next to my window but then relaxed in the same breath. I knew that face like I knew the stars in the sky. "Redmond! You idiot!"

"Just lightening the moment. There's only the fence. But as far as I can tell, they don't expect a Burner from outside wanting to get in. I saw a few guards and sentries, but nothing more. But there's a weak spot. The forest is dense at the northwest corner. We can head in there."

I clutched his hand. The night was racing toward my heart, but I wouldn't give up. I was here, doing the right thing. "Mond?"

He looked at me with raised eyebrows.

"Can we wait until tomorrow? At dawn?"

He nodded with understanding. He slipped into the car and pulled me to him. It was about midnight and we needed our sleep. But really, we needed to delay just a bit longer in order for our courage to come back. It was always easier to feel optimistic in the morning. We spent the night in each other's arms. I woke with a flash before the sky even lightened. It was time.

And I was ready.

"Shall we?" I asked.

Redmond nodded. I got out of the car and we headed in. No real plan. We would sneak. We would find the others. We would win the day.

Or die trying.

CHAPTER 32

ear Diary,

I remember the facility, and here's what I know. It's a gigantic W-shaped building with three main parts and one main entrance. In the back is the play area, surrounded by barbed wire like a cage. It has grass and a basketball court. There is plenty of space to run.

In the front—I only saw it on my way out—there is a huge parking lot with all types of cars. Each leg of the W holds rooms with bunk beds in rows. But near the main entrance there's an almost hotel-like atmosphere with single rooms for guests.

And there are a whole lot of guests staying there at certain times. I don't know what makes it popular for Breathers. You'd think they'd grab the money they get from bringing a Burner in and get a mansion or something. I know some do. But a whole lot like staying close to the facility, as if it's home for them too.

Then again, like the Rider that had his home in the suburbs, a lot move on. I wonder what the difference is. Maybe it's not home. Maybe the Breathers are as trapped in the facility as I was. I wonder if they even have much choice in how they live their lives.

Oh, yeah, Farrell does. He likes it. But I wonder about a lot of them. I can't help wondering what makes my enemy tick.

But I guess it's good that a lot of Breathers live at the same facility I did. Get rid of the facility, get rid of a whole lot of the enemy. If I could get rid of the facility. Great, I'm wandering again. This is supposed to be just the facts. I'll never see it again, or the others.

So, construction material. I guess concrete. The outside wall is thick concrete. I don't know the internal stuff. The inside floors are made of linoleum. There is definitely indoor plumbing. Water through pipes could be useful. I could freeze them. But then what?

The inside left of the W has a barracks of sorts with beds, but maybe it's more like a dorm. There are bathrooms every twenty feet. In the rooms, there are bunk beds against the walls, two sets per room.

Near the exit to the play yard, a door leads to the library, where racks and racks of books wait for the eager mind. A few computers—no internet. Maybe they didn't want us to be able to contact the outside world. Maybe our powers are dangerous for people to know about. I don't know.

I know there's a lab where they do some cutting up after the deaths. I've only seen the lab once, when Belinda died. I saw the place they took her. But there's another area, down the last leg of the W. At the very end, there's a room that is for... Well, whatever they did to kill Belinda. I've never seen that room, and that's a very good thing. End of the line.

And, of course, there's a morgue. What they do with our bodies after we're dead is a mystery.

There's, of course, one more area I have never seen. Outside the W there's a humongous building like a greenhouse. All one-sided glass. I don't know what's inside, but I know they don't grow plants there. Who knows what they do grow.

Forest surrounds the facility with only one long and winding road inside. A security gate starts the road. And a whole lot of fence borders the entire three-acre area. Maybe I could freeze that fence. If I wanted to. If I wanted to save everyone. But there are guards who patrol the perimeter.

I'd never make it.

The facility holds my friends, my family.

And I'll never save them.

CHAPTER 33

Redmond burned a hole through the fence. Yes, he was Redmond again. Mond was for heaven, for peace. This was war. We slipped through the hole and slowly ran from tree to tree. We had spent so much time planning and strategizing that noon was coming close as we walked through the forest that surrounded the facility. I kept my backpack on. I couldn't leave it behind. The stuff inside was some of the most important in my life. Before Redmond, it was *the* most important stuff in my life. The sun blasted overhead. It was much too warm for a winter sun; I guess spring was coming. And with it, the birthdays of quite a few of the older girls.

"That tree," Redmond hissed, nodding toward one fat tree in particular. We scurried behind it. I tried to twist my ears in half, ready for anything. The forest floor was covered in dead, dry leaves. Every crunch was like the sound of bones under my feet. Of my death. Of Redmond's.

My breath was loud in my ears, as was my heartbeat. This was different from what I had done before. I had run and hid. Now I was heading in.

On our next trip around a tree, we came face to face with a Breather.

We froze. He froze, quite literally . I snapped my fingers on pure instinct and an ice block surrounded him. It didn't touch him, so he couldn't absorb it. No direct attack. Got that from Redmond.

He was alive, banging against the wall of ice. I lifted my arms up and another ice block surrounded the previous one.

"Laoni." Redmond let out an impressed whistle. "How are you doing that?"

"Moisture in the air. Humidity's a bitch," I said and tried to throw my arm up again. But Redmond caught it.

"Stop. He's subdued. At least for a while."

"I want him to suffocate," I said. My tone tasted bitter.

"Maybe he will. But you'll be out. I want you with me for this. I need you."

My anger evaporated. We turned our backs on the enemy and slipped again from tree to tree. We weren't unfortunate enough to come face to face with another Breather. We managed to get to the inside yard. I saw the fence that I had been way too used to. I had taken it for normal when I played outside. I was in prison, and yet I never realized it.

"So, nice place," Redmond whispered as I stood frozen under the base of a large elm.

"A place like this was my home. I played tetherball right there," I said with a point to the grassy yard and its currently abandoned pole. "I lived and grew up waiting for slaughter."

Redmond clutched my shoulders. "Laoni, keep it together. Where is everyone? What are they doing?"

I had no watch. None worked around my icy wrists. I glanced at the sun. "I think it's noon. We got a chance to play around two. If they are on the schedule they had when I was locked up, everyone is at lunch. They're together. That makes things easier. I do love when luck is on my side."

Redmond shook his head so vigorously he moved my hand. Oh, he was holding my hand. This stupid facility had made me immune to his touch. Well, almost. The fear the facility instilled in me, the memory of running from it, expecting a Breather on my tail… It all took precedence in my mind.

"This isn't luck. This is the right path. Something out there wants us to succeed. Just like when I happened to come across you before I…"

I forced a smile. "Great. We're protected, aren't we?"

Redmond shrugged. He brought my hand upward for a kiss. "It's mysterious. And unpredictable. And bad things do happen. I know. But I wholeheartedly believe that when luck is with you, you'll find the right path. We're on the right path."

I bit my lip. I couldn't put down his optimism. But this path wasn't going to be easy, and there was a real chance both of us would be dead by the end of the day. Some luck!

"Okay," I said, instead of what I was thinking. "If we go in at the bottom of the middle line of the W, we'll go straight through the lunchroom. If you burn and keep burning, surrounding us with whatever flame you can manage, I can get to the others and usher them out. We run back out the same way." I halted as a thought hit. "Umm…"

"What is it?"

I turned toward him. My expression made his mouth fall open. "We don't have room in the Ferrari for twenty people! Why didn't we think about that?"

Redmond opened his mouth, but then closed it again. He thought quickly. "We'll have to do some modifications. The top can be sheared off. Everyone will have to get very close, very fast. Hey, it's better than staying here to die."

I was very careful to count to ten before I responded. "That won't work. We'll need a bus." I shot my eyes toward the parking lot. Well, well, well, it looked like Redmond's luck theory was true. A big old city bus was parked near the back of the lot. It'd fit us easily.

"Redmond," I said slowly. "There's a bus. Can you get to it and remain unseen? Drive it backward to this area?" I pointed to the fenced-in yard. I swear I was going to barf up all the meals I had yesterday.

"But you need me to get inside the facility."

"There's running water inside. Underground pipes. That's me. But I can't drive, nor can I hotwire a bus. We'll leave the Ferrari behind."

"Aww, man. I wanted a cool escape. What will those kids think of us?"

He was teasing, but I was so not in the mood. "Redmond…"

"You want me to shut up, got it."

I closed my eyes and leaned heavily against the tree.

"Laoni, are you okay?"

"I didn't want to do this alone. I didn't want to come back. You're the only reason I had hope. Now I have to go in alone. I can't do this."

I felt Redmond's hand on my chin. It crept around to my cheeks and brought my face up. When my eyes opened, his were inches away, his nose resting on mine. "You are the only one who could do this. Me? I hid. I survived. You fought. You conquered. You think you need me? The snow queen needs a stupid little flame?"

"That's not true."

He held up his finger between our eyes so I could see it. "No. Whatever you feel about me, thank you. I love you for it."

Suddenly, the facility wasn't there. There wasn't mortal danger around the corner. All I could feel was love!

"But don't waste your breath trying to get me to feel good

about myself. Point it at you. Give yourself the encouragement you need. Lives are counting on you."

I reached up to grab the back of his head and pulled him into a kiss. It was a heady, scary thing. Almost a goodbye. Almost a see you again real soon. His optimism was catching. "Redmond, I love you too."

His grin broke out. "That's good. Can't wait to get to the island so we can show each other again."

I hit the back of his head. "You, just focus."

Redmond held his hands up. "Hey, that's a great motivation for me. To be able to touch you again is all I want in this world."

I pointed at the facility. "Danger!" I reminded.

He gave me one of his irresistible smiles. One more kiss and we had to separate.

It was time to do as I had once planned but had never really intended.

I was going to break into the facility.

Millions of thoughts ran through my head. Should I run? Walk casually? Redmond was sneaking from tree to tree to get to the parking lot. I could see his form moving easily. But there was no cover where I was going. Should I crouch? Crawl on my belly?

Too much thinking. I finally just ran straight toward the building. The moisture in the air was lovely. I surrounded myself in an ice tunnel. Pillows of vapor surrounded me as I headed toward the wall. I felt for the pipes and found a bathroom. I concentrated on the water inside the pipes. In seconds, it was a frozen snake. Then I made it wiggle.

I heard the sounds of ripping material. I wriggled it like it was alive, trapped in the walls. It tore large chunks out with hissing noises.

I carved myself a passage.

Suddenly, my ice tunnel exploded around me. I wasn't even inside the facility!

I shot my eyes upward. Oh. Crap. In. the. Morning.

The third kind of Breather hovered above me. Her eyes glowed red. A Flyer. A freaking Flyer had seen me!

Thank goodness Redmond wasn't here. Maybe he could still escape.

The metal tentacles shot from the Breather's shoulders and twisted around me.

CHAPTER 34

*D*iary, *this is a new chapter of my life. I like it, I think. I'm free. I don't know what to do. I'm only twelve! I've lost my friends, my family. But I've lost Farrell too. He let me go. No, I escaped him. It doesn't matter that he was in a car and I was on foot. He should have caught me. Maybe he still will.*

No. Breathe. Ugh. No, can't. No, no, no. Stop it! You're fine. Inhale. Exhale. Got it. I'm on my own. I headed south. I sneaked onto buses and got pretty far. I think I saw a sign saying "Welcome to Virginia," but I don't know where that is. I don't know where to go or if I should stay.

I miss everyone! I suddenly miss even Erin. I'm in a library. I asked an adult if I could stay with her for a few days. She actually said yes. She believed my story that my parents had been delayed on their flight and I have no key to my house.

Just remember, Diary and self, I can't touch her. If I touch her, she won't like me. She makes cookies.

*O*ops, sorry, Diary. I got distracted. I thought I saw Farrell outside, looking in on me. But it can't be. I lost him. I've got a plan. I'll just keep telling the "My parents are delayed, and I have no key" story until I'm old enough to get my own place.

Oh, the cookies are done. Gotta talk later. I have a home for a few nights at least.

~

*T*he lady's name is Dharma. She makes cookies and loves tuna sandwiches. And she lets me watch TV all I want. She's asking questions, though. I don't like them. I can't answer them truthfully, so I lie. I've caught her staring at me. I think she might call someone soon.

I've begged her not to. She agreed. I don't know if she's telling the truth, though. She is one of those "do the right thing" people. Not that I've met many, but I've read about them. Dharma thinks she can save the world. Save me. If she could just get me somewhere safe. She doesn't understand, she's the safest for me now. More news soon.

~

I don't know why I'm so jumpy. I'm watching this crime show where criminals are wanted but never found. It's making me think someone's outside. Ugh. I'm gonna talk to Dharma. She'll give me cookies. Then I'll go to bed. What IS that noise outside? Like a helicopter's blade, all chop, chop, chop. It's probably nothing.

~

iary... I want to cry. I can barely write. The lady's dead. That's right, dead. It wasn't Farrell. He wouldn't. It was another kind. A Breather that flies, that was more machine than anything else. I was...

I don't want to write this!

What am I doing? I thought I was safe. I was better off at the facility.

No. No. No. I wasn't. When I turn sixteen, I'm dead. Just like the nice lady.

I was in my bed. Stop it! I won't cry! Now I have to stay alive to honor the woman who jumped in front of me. She was too nice. I was in bed. The lady had pulled out a cot for me. I heard a whirring. A noise. It sounded like the roof was being eaten up.

The lady ran in, screaming. Then we both looked up.

This monstrosity was over us. The lady took a look at me and then jumped in front of me.

The thing grabbed her with this ugly metal tentacle and squeezed. She died.

I ran. She bought me precious seconds. I have to keep running.

I will survive for her. The one who died trying to protect me.

CHAPTER 35

I should have expected the Flyer, honestly. How could I forget? There were a lot of Burners about to give up energy. That would be a prize for anyone to take —or they might escape. Whatever. The extra security would be Flyers.

The Flyer had a tentacle around my throat, but she didn't tighten it. Instead, the other metal tentacles roared out and wrapped around me. But the Flyer didn't kill me. It just grabbed me and pulled me up into the air. My head spun as I hung there. But it whooshed down at a dizzying speed again before I could even try to get free. Overhead, the W section of the facility was a bit thicker than I had thought. In the center was a big square roof that opened to allow the Flyer to exit and enter.

The Flyer still held me tight. It said nothing, did nothing. I think she was made of flesh and blood, but there had been so many augmentations, she didn't look human anymore. A metallic sheen was under her skin. Her red eyes surrounded by silver glared at me like an angry traffic light.

"Let me go," I implored. What else could I do but beg? I

didn't know how Flyers worked. But maybe there was something better in them than the Runners, who were so happy to cause me pain.

"My orders are to hold you," the Flyer said. There was no emotion in that voice. It didn't even seem like a voice. If a silver hole could talk, this was what I imagined it would sound like.

"You don't care, though," I said. Was I talking to a computer? She was sliding back down toward the building. She had me tight. I had failed in my attempt to appeal to her better nature. Maybe Redmond could get the others out without me. This was why I had never come back. I couldn't do a thing. "Who are you?"

The Flyer turned to stare silver eyes into mine. "I am a Flyer. You are my prey. You will be brought to the prison. Do not struggle. Your end is nigh."

A whole lot of personality. Huh, I oddly preferred the Bloodhounds.

I didn't listen but continued to struggle. I had nothing to lose here. I pulled some ice blades and started hacking at the metal around my body, but the Flyer didn't whimper, didn't move. It just tightened the coils around my body.

"I am to bring you in unharmed. Struggle more, and I will be forced to knock you unconscious."

I stopped struggling. I could do nothing at the moment. But there might still be a chance to succeed. I couldn't give up. Redmond was relying on me. My family was relying on me.

The building came up quickly, gathering in size as we headed into it. The Flyer flipped to drop toward the open roof. I was back in the facility.

CHAPTER 36

he third Breather. The Flyers.

I haven't forgotten the fear Flyers give me. I haven't encountered them much. They were purely used for the most sensitive of security issues. The first one was after me because it...umm. She had thought I had been the one to break security and wanted to know why. But after that first one, I only saw a few.

Farrell had explained why during one of his monologues when he was about to let me run so the chase could continue. Flyers keep the peace. They go after Breathers or Burners who dare to make too many waves. No one could know about them. They weren't ruled by the same laws. When a Flyer was sent out, anyone getting in the way would die, as I can attest to.

These facts are the hardest to write. Not just because they scare the crap out of me, but because Flyers are so elusive. As far as I have figured out, they aren't sent out a lot. They have no trouble killing humans, unlike the Runners and the Riders. I'm not sure they balk at anything.

I think they're programmed to kill, like machines. If they are alive, they have no conscience.

Okay, technical details. They all have these little holes on their backs right under their shoulder blades where yards and yards of coiled tentacles are stored.

Flyers have red eyes. I'm not sure exactly how they fly. Maybe rocket propulsion from their feet? But I've only heard the sound of a helicopter when they arrive, and not even that sometimes. It's as if some are silent and some want you to hear that they're coming. They always wear these really ugly black suits. Everything else about them is terrifyingly normal.

Oh, except for their mouths. When they smile, if they smile, their teeth are shown. There are only four, top and bottom. All blunt and flat. I wonder what they eat.

Check that, I don't want to know.

The first two kinds of Runners and Riders have the ability to breathe in a Burner's powers, but I don't know about the Flyers. I've never even tried to attack them. I've run every time I've seen one.

As far as personality goes, they don't have much. I know the Runners I've met always seem to have this sadistic joy in chasing me. The Riders, too. But the Flyers don't seem to care one way or another.

Which makes me wonder how they come about. I mean, I know that the Breathers are bred. They're young at one point. I assume there are baby Runners and Riders somewhere. But what about Flyers? I can't imagine one ever being a baby.

I don't know their weaknesses.

I don't know how to kill one.

CHAPTER 37

I heard the clicks of metal shoes in the hallway in front of me. The tentacles around me gripped me so tightly, I almost fainted when I saw who it was.

Digory had survived. He grinned when our eyes met. "Hello, beautiful. It's been a while." He nodded to the Flyer. "You can let her go. There is *really* no place for her to run."

"As you wish." The Flyer clicked and the tentacles around me slid back into her shoulders. Then the ceiling opened up and she flew upward again.

I just stood there. Digory was right. There was nowhere for me to go. I was right back in the very place I had escaped from years and years ago.

Digory didn't look too good, though. The fire had done its damage. His skin was red and torn in many places, and some of it just didn't exist anymore. Most of his hair had burnt off, leaving half of his head bald. In fact, he kinda looked like Darth Vader when he removed his helmet and disappointed the hell out of me when I found out he wasn't James Earl Jones.

"That must have hurt," I said. My fear was far off. I mean,

the worst-case scenario just happened. What more did I have to fear?

Digory lost his sadistic smile as he patted his head. "It did at that. But we Breathers are a resilient sort. It'll heal. I'll be as fit as a fiddle in about a year. Something I can't say about you."

"What about that Rider caught in the flames with you?" Not that I was actually concerned.

"Him? Well, he did go up like a bonfire. I roasted marshmallows as he screamed. He is dead."

"Nice." The loyalty, or lack of it, never surprised me.

"So, welcome home. This is like your home, right?"

"Never." I wasn't going to admit anything to him. "I was kidnapped and forced to stay."

"Semantics. Look, Laoni. That is your name, right?"

I just stood there. I felt for any water nearby. Anything I could use. But this place was dry. There weren't even any pipes in the walls. I couldn't attack directly. It wouldn't hurt him.

"Laoni, your friends have missed you. Why not pop in and see them? Tell them how you've been in a wonderful place that all Burners go when they reach sixteen. They have been a bit…hard to control as of late."

I smiled. Of course! Erin—cynical, moody, distrusting— would never have accepted the passing years with ease. "And you want me to assure them everything will be fine."

He shrugged. "It will be. Every single day, more and more Burners are discovered. I can't have them hearing the legend of Laoni, the one who escaped. They share ghost stories about the dead Belinda. It wasn't like this before your escape. The children were happy. They grew and formed into great energy."

"Die," I ordered. "Then get revived. Then die again." I crossed my arms. "And then repeat."

Digory didn't look so jovial anymore. He snapped his fingers. As if from smoke, two Breathers slipped in behind me. They were so close I jumped away, but I only bumped into Digory. He shot his hand out and grabbed me by the throat. He yanked my backpack off and slipped it onto his shoulder.

"Mine now," he said with mockery in his voice. "Now, Laoni, me asking is a courtesy. The only reason you're still alive is because you have caused anarchy in this once peaceful facility."

I gagged as he tightened his fingers around my throat. "I won't… I won't…do it."

He released my throat, and I fell to the floor.

"I wanted to do this the nice way. You will tell them. You can be covered in bruises or not. It's your choice."

A booted foot caught me between my shoulder blades. I betrayed myself and let out a whimper. That hurt! He wouldn't get another peep out of me, I swore. I calmly kept my eyes on his as he punched his knuckles into my ribcage and then again into my stomach.

"Let us help," the Breathers with him cooed.

"Well, Laoni?" he asked. "Care to rethink your decision?"

I pushed myself to standing. I moved closer to him. Even now, his eyes widened in the awe of my beauty. I guess my anger made me even more impressive.

Then I spit right into his face. It was a sharp little ice ball. It left a thin, red cut on his face on top of his burns. He screamed out. His yell seemed to spur the others on. Suddenly, I was being punched and kicked by three men. One got me in the ribs, the other in the head.

Black took my vision. But I heard Digory say, "No, you don't. You won't escape that way."

He shook me back awake. "Back with us?"

I tried to spit again, but he covered my mouth. "Good." Then he punched me again.

"Did you know that your blood runs warm? Amazingly, it doesn't freeze. And it makes you even more beautiful." Then he brought a cuff into my nose. My face exploded with pain.

I still didn't cry out. "You…feel…like a fly landing on my face. What a weakling. I've…been punched harder. Much harder."

He growled and grabbed me by the hair. "Fine! You want pain? You'll get it. If you don't ease the worries of this facility, then the fear your dead body will bring will still keep order. No!" That was to the other Breathers. "She's mine. I'm taking her to the energy gatherer."

"We all get the reward," one hissed. "I'm almost free."

That echoed in my head. Something to focus on rather than its throbbing. Free… So they too were trapped. I didn't feel sorry for them, but it added more to the info in my head. They did it for more than just money. I wondered, was that life in a home that the Rider had their reward? A life away from the facility?

Digory shook me. I was barely standing. "I don't care that much about the reward. I just want her. I'll enter your names into the computer as well as mine."

They let him go. He dragged me through the hallway. "Ah, poor little boy doesn't get his way," I said. Inside, I wondered what it'd feel like to die. That's where I was headed. Even if I could figure out how to get out from this place I had never been, I wasn't sure I could fight off anyone in my current state. The Breathers had hit me hard.

Even now, my head throbbed. My ribs hurt. I wondered what a broken arm felt like because I was holding my arm at a funny angle. All this was so far away. I had one thought. I wouldn't let him win any more than he had already.

"Stop it!" Digory yelled. "You are supposed to be beaten! Defeated! How can you smile?"

I then noticed that my mouth was making an upward movement. My split lip complained, but it was just one pain among many. "Because you can hurt me physically, you may even kill me, but you can't win. You'll never have my mind. I'm not afraid of you."

He stopped dragging me and pushed me against the wall. He crept up to my face and ran one finger down my cheek. "I don't want fear. I want your body."

I almost laughed. This Breather was an idiot. "Umm, you do know what will happen if you try anything with me, right?"

He grabbed my chin and made my lips pucker. "I will have fun."

I pulled my face out of his grip. "No, moron. You'll freeze to death."

He scoffed. He leaned his body against mine. Shoving my back harder into the hard wall. "Really? Like your powers have done so well against me in the first place."

I think I actually had to roll my eyes. "My powers are abnormal. But the stuff inside me—all of it—is me. And as you experienced with the fire…" I worked through a stiff arm to put my hand up to his face and flick a hanging piece of flesh. "That normal stuff hurts. Can you imagine what it'll do if you put other body parts inside frozen places?"

He pulled away. Disappointment covered his face. I was safe in that way, at the very least. He wouldn't risk it.

He yanked me onward, harder now. "If I could, I'd have fun with other things with your body. Sharp knives wouldn't freeze," he said.

"But you don't have time. Your masters are calling, doggy. Better be a good boy."

He growled, but I knew I was right. He had to either

recruit me or kill me. Something was going on in this facility. I had assumed that Farrell and all the Breathers were in charge. But they weren't. There was someone above them. Someone who pulled all the strings.

All these years I had spent fearing my return, imagining coming back as the savior, I had forgotten how much Erin hated it here. I wondered if she could get in touch with Redmond. Maybe they could help each other.

For my part, it looked like I was going out. Every step sent sharp blades of pain into my entire body. The hallway was long, but there was a room at the end. It had one big black door with a fingerprint identifier to let a person in.

Digory shoved me through the door.

And I finally saw it. The place where Belinda had been taken.

The place where Burners died.

A metal floor spread out underneath a huge machine. There were no windows. Six people were waiting. All of them wore lab coats, a stark contrast to the dark metal walls. And they were all human. Not one was a Breather. They knew about me! They had asked me to be brought here.

One looked toward me. "She fought back, I take it?"

"She never does anything but," he snapped and shoved me forward. The guy caught me and pushed me onto a table. It was attached to a huge gaping hole in the machine. Inside was dark, but I saw some weird hanging things with what looked like needles on the end.

Okay, the machine looked like one of those MRI scanning machines. The little bed would be pulled inside. But this one wasn't the same. The imposing darkness inside didn't help people feel better. I'd feel much, much worse being put into this thing.

The others held my wrists and legs as they strapped me down. They needn't have bothered. I was done. All these years I spent running only to run back and finally get captured. That had to be a punishment for leaving my friends behind. For not believing Erin sooner. If I had, maybe Belinda would still be alive.

Maybe we all would.

"She is so beautiful," one murmured from my left. "She's crying icy tears. I can't...I need to touch her. She is...so *beautiful!*"

I heard a lot of shuffling as the one who said these things was stopped before grabbing me. "Get him out of here," Digory ordered.

The said man was subsequently dragged from the room. Not in a violent way. In fact, I heard words of encouragement and friendship.

"We've all been there, Phil. They're inhumanly beautiful, but it'll pass. Just fight it, come on. Don't give in to her pull."

I was left with Digory and three others.

"He's new," Digory said next to my head.

I ignored him. I closed my eyes and went away. There was no reason to be here. Not when an innocent—well, maybe innocent—girl on a table is given less sympathy than a monster who would kill her. What was the use in this world? In me?

From far away, I felt the table sliding into the dark hole. The needles were on mechanical arms. I could hear whirring noises as they stabbed willy-nilly into whatever part of my body they wanted. Little stinging pains shot through my body. But, like my lip, they were just small pains among larger ones.

I could still hear Digory. "She'll hurt, right? I want to hear her scream. The little creature only whimpered once."

"Oh, she'll scream," the other voice said. I was in darkness. I could only feel the sharp jabs of the needles inside my flesh. "Not a creature on this earth can fight the urge to stay alive. She'll beg. She'll cry. She'll wriggle like a worm on a hook. I always find it quite wonderful. These abominations sound quite human when they die."

The room smelled like fear despite his sadistic words. He was scared of me. He wanted me and my kind wiped off the face of the earth. Well, right now I wanted the same, but for him.

Anger burned through me, wiping out the guilt I would have held onto. Didn't Belinda go through this very same thing? And no one saved her. She couldn't save herself.

But my anger had always burned the same way. Hot. My wrist was trapped. I guess they thought that would make me safe. *Hey, idiots, I've been on the run for four years.*

I've learned stuff.

And these were humans. Not Breathers.

I snapped my fingers. I kept my eyes closed even as I heard the scream. I had brought up a shard of ice and just let it shoot from my fingers. Guess I hit someone.

"You moron!" Digory yelled. "You were in her way."

"I didn't know!"

I couldn't help it. It was probably stupid. But I still said, "Guess you scream too, huh? Yet you do it when a little pain shoots your way, not when you're about to die. How cowardly is that?"

I heard his hand slam on something. The machine turned on.

"You can't do it on that high of a setting," another complained. He sounded amused, though. He wasn't the one who had been hit.

"I don't care. The bitch attacked me! Kill it!"

Ah, those words took me back. Mom screaming as I was dragged away. Not protecting me. Too afraid.

Slimy energy surrounded me. Every needle in my skin didn't put something in, it dragged out. Something inside me. My back arched. Was my very skin being turned inside out? My core was melting, bleeding.

No, I wouldn't scream. I knew what was happening.

I was being robbed of who I was. The very makeup of my skin and bones. Everything was being taken away.

Inside, I whimpered. It wasn't fire. It wasn't ice. It was both. Frozen to death. Burned alive. Every fiber of my being twisting and pulling—stripped.

Then it increased.

That was just the beginning.

I didn't want to scream.

I was going to.

The bastard was right. I had no choice. My body wanted to emit the cry that refused to believe what was happening to it.

No! My mouth was opening. I wouldn't! I wouldn't let them win!

Then everything stopped. The pain was gone.

Well, most of it. The pain from the needles was still there, and the rest of my body ached. But the major pain was gone. I was quivering all over. I don't know what, if anything, had been taken from me.

My ears rushed and roared, but finally, I heard the conversation.

"An energy outage? That's impossible. We have a generator. A backup generator."

The darkness seeped into my vision. I only could hear. The roaring in my ears subsided. I only felt the pain in my arm and ribs now. Everything was coming back. My ice wasn't gone. But what did I feel on my head? Sweat? Was my body actually trying to cool down?

Nothing made any sense, but the pain still coursed through my veins. And I was still angry.

I pulled any water I had at my disposal. My own sweat. I

shot it like bullets through the machine above me. I shredded it. I sat up and yanked the needles from my skin. Then I crawled out of my torture chamber. I saw shadowy figures banging around, trying to get the machine back to work.

They couldn't see me. There was no light.

But any minute now, their electricity would be back on. They would put me back in that thing if it still worked. I had no more sweat. What an anomaly! It was gone as fast as it had come, a reaction to the machine. I had been losing everything.

Water, water, where are you?

"She's out!" the same voice as before yelled.

"We can't get her energy. Shoot her." I heard the slide of metal on some kind of table, the click of a gun being readied.

So cruel, so cold. So was I.

I found the water I needed. Inside bodies. I could do a lot with it, but there was more deeper down. "You really shouldn't have drunk so much liquid today," I said. I put my hand into a fist, then I opened it. I heard screams all around me as their bladders burst. Maybe it was a good thing it was so dark. I didn't want to see this carnage no matter how much they all deserved it.

Again, I was killing with no mercy. Maybe I was a monster.

"Now, was that totally necessary?" Digory asked next to my ear. He grabbed my arms and twisted them behind my back. "Sure, they were annoying, but they were far from the only ones in charge. Now what should we do with you?"

I struggled, but Digory was pushing me to the ground.

"No, no, let's just stay here until they get the lights back on. There are more Breathers around the corner and stupid humans. So, let's just stay right here until you get what you deserve."

I couldn't use his water the same way as the humans. I could do nothing without water. He put his knee between my shoulder blades and pinned me down.

Damn it! I was so sick of feeling helpless!

Then amazing things happened. A loud swell of noise roared through the facility. We could hear it even in here.

People were screaming everywhere. The door slammed open, and a voice called, "Anyone in here?" I didn't recognize the voice. It sounded human.

Digory released some of the pressure on me to answer. "Yeah, me and the Burner. What's up?"

"Digory! Can I hide in here? The Burners have gone mad. They're attacking everything that moves. Fire is burning. The generators have been melted to a puddle."

I smiled even with my face pushed against the floor. Redmond! He had stayed. He had done the siege he wanted. Wow, oh wow, was he good. Then again, he had help.

"You're doomed," I said. I pushed up so suddenly that he rolled off of me. I stood up and saw the outline of another human. "Hey, Diggie, do you think this human has enough liquid for me to use?"

"Hey, no!" he yelled and was gone before I could even threaten again.

"Guess not." I punched my fist as hard into Digory's nose as I could. I felt the satisfying crunch of bones breaking. "Now, I'm going to leave, Breather. I'm going to join my friends and we are going to walk out of here. You will never follow us again. You will never see us again."

Digory's shadowy form was holding his hand to his nose. "You have nowhere to go. There are facilities all over the place like this. You'll never be free. See, we have the humans on our side. I'll find you again."

I slammed my hands into a flat, palm-down position.

Droplets of blood from the bodies at my feet surrounded me. I formed them into cold and sharp icicles. "You won't."

Then I impaled him. I killed another Breather, this time with hundreds of sharp blades again and again. I will never forget his dying screams. His threats got pretty inventive.

But I was done running. I didn't even wait for his lifeless body to fall to the floor. I just felt around for my backpack and found its lumpy shape on a table near the exit.

By feel, I made my way out of the room. "That was for you, Belinda," I whispered to the dark room I left behind. In the hall, I could see a little better. Windows let in the light of the day.

Everything was chaos. The facility I knew so well was under attack. Walls were missing. People were running. I went toward the source of the commotion.

It was in the lunchroom. The hallways leading there were the emptiest. Outside, I could see the humans and Breathers gathering together, trying to bring their side of the war up, I guess.

War. Well, it was about time.

CHAPTER 38

This entry will be about the friends I left behind. I won't forget them.

I'll start with Erin because she's the most annoying. She has this really long black hair that frizzes out around her head like a cloud. But it's a beautiful cloud. She's gorgeous, like all of us. I think she's from Florida, but I'm not sure which city. I've never been good with geography. She used to tell me, between conspiracy theories, about her life before she was brought to the facility. Unlike me, she was taken from a family that loved her. Farrell kidnapped her right out of her bed. She loves dogs, but only big kinds, and she wants to be—wanted to be—a pilot. She's smart, mouthy, and gets angry easily.

Cindy, my former shadow, is from New Mexico. Her family moved there from Kyoto, Japan, long ago. Cindy thinks they're insane to have given up all the beauty of Kyoto for the dusty streets of a place called Los Lunas, New Mexico, but they were in love with the idea of America and thought New Mexico would be a nice place. Cindy let me know she had hated it. She actually likes the facility because it has green grass. But she misses her parents and sister immensely. I don't know what she's doing there without me. I was kinda her family. Now I'm gone. She keeps losing family.

Then there's Mandy. She's an ice controller too, but she doesn't show it. I'm not even sure how Farrell found her. Her skills are latent, I guess. Her parents are homeless. Or were, I guess. Thanks to the money Farrell gave them for Mandy, they probably bought a nice house.

Bobby is one of those shy, quiet types who always stares off into space, existing in another world. At least, he was when he arrived at the facility. He has blond hair that fades into his scalp. Even his eyebrows are blonde. He likes only one thing, and that's bugs. One time a ladybug flew into the yard and he spent an hour talking about it. Where it sleeps, eats, and even more boring things. It was the only time I heard him talk in more than monosyllabic grunts. While I was studying languages in the library, he would be looking up bugs. He thought they were neat. And since I was his study buddy, he thought I was neat. He was my friend, I guess. I'm not sure if I was as good a friend as he was to me.

Frankie is explosive. He wants to be a performer on Broadway one day. I think he might grow into his looks, but currently, his face is really long and his forehead is tiny. I'm not sure if it's an effect of his Burner status or not, but his hair doesn't grow. It's always just peach fuzz on top of his head. I like it, but he won't stop wearing hats.

Kenya is the nice one. I can't believe how beautiful she is. Long brown hair that never needs brushing, really dark brown eyes, and the curliest eyelashes I have ever seen. She always asks if anyone wants juice, even when we're in the middle of playing in the yard. She always waits to sit at lunch, and if someone's behind in her in line, she begs them to go in front of her.

Jeff has a baby face. It's much rounder than the rest of ours. It's because of this that he acts like he's much older. He was two years younger than me when he was brought in, but from the moment he accepted that he wasn't going anywhere and no one was coming to *pick him up, he has taken to starting his sentences with, "Now children." No one listens to him. And if there's a prank to be played, it's usually on him.*

Those are the ones I can actually remember. The other thirteen formed their own groups, and we only really saw each other across the yard. But they were all like me.

With one exception. I'll live. They won't.

CHAPTER 39

As I slipped into the lunchroom, fire fizzled against me. Across the room, I saw someone I hadn't in years.

"Erin, you've changed." And she had. Her dark brown hair, which used to fly around uninhibited, had been cut to a buzz. She looked more muscular. Under her white, spaghetti-strap top, her muscles were taut in strong lines. She was, of course, much taller, but she looked like some kind of warrior goddess, fire burning on her fingertips. Both she and Cindy were lounging on the lunch tables while others were running back and forth, looking out the windows or just causing a mess.

"Nice shirt." I gestured to her obviously non-regulation clothes.

"Thanks. Made it myself. Lets my powers out. I like yours too. Oh, and I've been waiting to see you again. I have something to say to you."

I had to smile. "What's that?"

"Told you so."

I pursed my lips. "You did. What's going on?"

"Revolution!" Cindy said. She too had changed. What was going on here? Both Erin and Cindy were *fit*. An aerobics instructor would envy their forms. Cindy's dark, black hair was also cut short, and her broad forehead was free of the bangs I was used to. "I knew you'd be back. Even when they moved us across the country, I knew. One day."

I'm glad she was so sure. I wasn't. I walked closer and scooted onto the table to sit next to them.

Erin shot me a glance. "You cut it pretty close, though. I think I was going to be dragged off tomorrow."

"I wasn't sure… What is this anyway?"

"We heard your attack. It was time for us."

Cindy slapped hands with me. "Erin's been planning it since you and Belinda disappeared. But she said, 'Showtime' when we heard the pipes breaking. She sounded so cool. Like an army general on TV."

"Oh, shut up," Erin said, but she hid a smile. "I knew something would happen today. The stars were in alignment."

I grinned. She believed in stars, but not humans.

"Did you do the blackout? Because it was awesome!"

I shrugged. Then Erin's gaze followed my wounded form. "What happened to you? Is that an ice cast?"

I looked down. I had been so out of it, I hadn't even remembered the Breathers had broken my arm. "Oh, yeah, I guess it is."

"Oh, she's got skills!" Cindy yelled. "Anyway, so Erin turned super or whatever, and then we attacked. Ever since you left, we have been removing those restrictive clothes they gave us when they weren't looking and practicing with our powers. So, when Erin said, 'It's showtime'…"

"Would you stop?" Erin groaned.

"We started attacking everything that moved. But it was

when the electricity went out that they really started freaking out. The staff ran. The Breathers thought it to be an attack from outside, so they regrouped outside. Now, we're just waiting for the next step."

"What do we do?" Erin asked.

Me. She asked me, of all people. Like she wasn't doing fine on her own. Like she hadn't been doing fine during all the years I'd lived in a sewer like a rat. I said nothing in response. Maybe if I waited long enough, she would take control again.

But I was wrong. All that did was make them both give me a long look.

"You're bleeding," Cindy said worriedly.

"She probably had to take out a few on the way in," Erin soothed.

I again didn't answer. I actually took them on the way out. Out of that machine that would have killed me if the electricity hadn't gone out. I didn't know what to do here. By my count, we were surrounded outside by a whole lot of Breathers and one Burner. But inside, all we had were Burners who trained while no one was looking. And me. Fat lot of good that did.

And that wouldn't be enough. I had trained for four years to survive and it barely saved me.

"We have force in numbers," Erin said, almost as if she could read my thoughts. "There are at least thirty kids still here."

"There were twenty when I left. So, they got ten more?"

Erin's face crumpled. "No. They brought in a hundred in the last four years, but they were older. All of them have already 'graduated.' Whatever. Anyway, what's left is us. And we're good. Lots of firepower."

Something I had never had. But it wasn't enough. I bit my split lip. "Um, you attacked the Breathers?"

"Not directly! We're not that stupid." Erin moaned. "We learn fast. All around, use what's there." She was fired up by the heat of battle, ready to do something different than sitting and waiting. I, on the other hand, wasn't too jazzed by the idea of all these Burners dying when the very reason I was here was to save them. "We got that point when we were picked up. I didn't exactly come here without a struggle."

I almost smiled at the young Erin in my mind, screaming and exploding all the way in. The Breather must have been quite annoyed by her way back when. "That makes things easier. When we escape, they won't track us."

Erin and Cindy shared a look. A communication I didn't understand.

"We're not running." Erin stood up and slid off the table. "We've spent these years waiting for revenge."

I didn't answer. I couldn't. It's better to spend years waiting for revenge than on the run, wondering if the next minute would be your last. "You *are* running. That's what we're going to do."

Erin gasped with fire in her breath as she stood me down. I looked back. I felt calm, collected. I no longer had to fear anything but losing everyone. And I wouldn't. By some luck, I was still alive. I survived. Again. That's what we all had to do. Somehow, we all had to get back to the Mountain Lady and call for that submarine again.

Suddenly, a voice boomed all around us. Loud enough for a speaker, but nothing like one. A Breather's voice. A new skill I'd have to add to my diary.

"Burners, this is madness," he said. I didn't recognize the voice, but Erin gritted her teeth.

"Paul," she hissed. "Only a tad better than Digory."

"Digory's dead." I didn't add that I had killed him, but Cindy and Erin got the point real fast. New respect shined in their eyes even as Paul's voice boomed around our ears.

"We can and will kill all of you. You think your paltry powers can defeat us? Give up now and you won't suffer. But I promise that if you don't, I will personally torture every single one of you on the way to your death."

Ah, he was holding nothing back. The illusion that everyone was safe here had disappeared. All the Burners were listening, but somehow in my absence Erin had gotten to them all. They knew what awaited them in that room, and they were willing to fight to get away from that future.

I wondered three things in that moment. Had Redmond gotten the bus? Could he get here if I sent him some kind of message? How long would the Breathers outside wait for us to come out?

"Erin, do you trust me at all?"

She locked eyes with me. "Don't tell me to run."

"No. Straight on attack. Grab everything that's burning and surround them. Fire Burners, control the natural fires and send everything you've got. Ice Burners, it's a little more difficult for you."

What the hell was I doing? Just seconds ago, I wanted Erin to do what she needed to do. I wanted someone else to make these decisions. But now, I was ordering everyone around. Because I knew we'd never win this. I'd barely survived all those years. We needed to get out of there. It was all coming into place. I had been trained to do this since I first ran. All I had to do was accept my role as leader. And I would. I was done with running from who I needed to be. I was going to save them like Belinda had asked me to do so long ago.

"You can do direct attacks with any water around you, but it takes your energy. You can do a lot more with your powers against the humans, but that doesn't work against Breathers. I'm betting the humans will stay out of this war."

One by one, they lined up in front of me, faces turned up,

staring, ready for my command. I was the only one on the table now, standing, and these Burners, my troops, were looking to me for leadership.

Yay for me. I was going to tell them to run.

"You will wear out too quickly if you use your own powers. So, I'm thinking you stay near the building as the backup artillery. Use the water inside the pipes, inside the ground."

"Ah," Cindy whined. "I wanted to be at the head with Erin."

"Will you listen to me?" I asked sternly. "I've only killed three Breathers. Actually…" My eyes shot to every face, staring them down, taking command. A place I never wanted. "That's a question I'm asking all of you. You have a leader in Erin."

She smiled but looked embarrassed.

"She's gotten you this far. I won't force you to accept me. I can barely accept myself." I whispered that last part. "So, if you want me, say yay, and if not say nay."

A burst of yays hit my ears. They wanted me all right. The mythical girl who'd escaped. The one who'd come back for them. The hero that had been a coward. All they cared about was that I was back for them. They had no clue that if it weren't for Redmond, I'd be on a submarine to an island now.

"Then follow my orders. Erin?"

"What?" she asked. She had both arms crossed and scratched them in unison. She was nervous.

"What about you? Will you listen to me? I have a place we can all go. Belinda was right—about everything."

Erin's throat tightened as she swallowed. "Give the orders. I'll follow you wherever."

I stepped down and clasped her shoulder and then whispered in her ear, "It'll require running."

She just nodded.

The battle plan was set. I just had to hope Redmond had taken our battle as a signal to bring the bus around and not as an invitation to join in.

I also hoped he was still alive.

CHAPTER 40

*D*iary,
This is the last entry I will write. I'm catching a big breath before we charge forth. Either because I'll be dead after this battle or because I'll be too busy being free. We're waiting for the right time to attack. Paul is outside, still yelling. He's telling us all the things we can expect if we don't surrender. I sent out Cindy alone to tell him we were surrendering, but that we needed an hour to get the point to everyone.

Erin is looking at me with equal parts awe and accusation. She doesn't like the fact that I would choose to send Cindy out alone. But I had to explain that the Breathers will think Cindy is harmless. She will deliver the message, and they will let her go.

Then, while they are gearing down, so to speak, we'll attack and catch them off guard. I am so glad Digory and Farrell aren't out there. They wouldn't fall for this. But Paul, according to Erin, is gullible. He wants to win so badly he'll take our ruse of surrender at face value.

I have to admit, right now, I'm distracted. Redmond fills my brain much the same as Cindy fills Erin's mind. What if he were captured? What if he's dead? I hadn't seen any proof of him since the electricity outage. What is he waiting for?

Could I trust that he followed my orders exactly? Or did he do what he has always done and acted impulsively?

Diary, here, I can be honest. I can't live if he's dead. I'm not even sure I'll have the strength to go down fighting. Put me in a machine, I'll fight against the natural urge to scream. Give me impossible odds, and I'll continue to fight.

Kill Redmond? I'll sink into the ground and I'll scream and scream and let them take me without a fight.

Melodramatic? Maybe. But, Diary, you know me better than anyone else. I love him. He is my other half. My fire that burns for me.

Erin is trying to look over my shoulder, but I won't let her see what I've written. She's barely changed. We've been catching up as we sit here, looking out the window and watching the Breathers start to relax. Cindy is back. Erin gave her a long hug.

Erin says that their lives were good. They had meals, games, toys. A stark contrast to my life. I had no real meals, just whatever I could pick up that would freeze the least and taste tolerable. My games were avoiding the Breathers.

I think I had one toy since I left. A puzzle I found on the ground. I lost it in the sewer waters.

Am I bitter? Yeah. Totally. If I had just stayed put, I would have had the peace they had. But then again, I'd be dead by now. Hmm, tough choice.

Oops. It's time. I am scared more than I've ever been. I won't show it. They will think I'm brave. But everything hurts.

The battle begins.

CHAPTER 41

The attack started with a bang, quite literally. Bobby had been making bombs. I guess he had moved past bugs. He threw a Molotov cocktail right into the group of Breathers. It was a bit satisfying to see them running for a change. I led the assault, though Cindy gave me a look that clearly asked what I was doing. I was an Ice Burner. Why wasn't I back with them?

Because I had a very good reason to be at the front, and it involved waiting. I really hoped I had the energy for this.

As it was, I threw up an ice shield to protect me. I encased my body and watched the battle. I had asked the Fire Burners to do as big a show as possible. I guess the years trapped in this facility helped because it was a show. Plumes of fire caught on anything flammable. I think Kenya was actually forming her fire into shapes of flowers that spun down and caught on trees, keeping their shape as they burned around the Breathers. It was an inferno. An inferno of ice and fire.

All the Ice Burners turned the water inside into ice rivers that poured toward the Breathers.

And they were retreating. Yes!

Come on, Redmond.

Everything was chaos, but we were winning. Maybe I had been overreacting. We were good enough on our own. We could just leave.

I was wrong.

Without any warning, bullets shot through the air. They caught Bobby in the arm. He fell and his fire disappeared. All around me, Fire Burners were falling. And then the sky darkened. The Flyers were over us. They shot from Burner to Burner, knocking them down.

"No!" It was time. I pushed my ice shield out and it stretched and froze over everyone. The Flyers beat against it. The bullets embedded in my wall. I shook and kept it up. If Redmond didn't come soon, I would die. And with me, the shield. The only protection.

"Erin! Get up, gather up everyone," I moaned.

"We were winning," she said, grimacing at her bloody leg. A bullet must have grazed her.

"We lost just by existing. They're stronger. We need to run. We all do."

Erin limped over to Kenya, who was on the ground. Erin pulled her to standing, but Kenya was woozy. I don't know where she got hit.

Everyone was standing. They grouped together in a cluster, afraid. They were just children against the evil of the world.

They hadn't grown up yet. I had to. "Come on, Redmond," I begged and pushed the ice wall toward the group of Breathers. They just grinned as it came closer. They knew they wouldn't be hurt. But that wasn't my intent. It was just a blockade. The Burners looked at me, wondering what else could be done.

I was starting to cry. This was hard. I was more than

weak. My arm hurt. My ribs swelled with pain. The machine still echoed around me. And Redmond wasn't coming. If he wasn't, he was dead.

That meant I was as good as dead.

A few more minutes, and everyone else would be dead too.

Suddenly, the screeching of tires roared into my ears. A bus swept aside the cage and spun sideways in front of all of us.

"Mond!" I yelled, beyond delirious with relief and happiness.

He swung open the door. "Sorry I'm late, but they really didn't like me melting their generator. I had to fight a bit. Well, everyone, this is the next bus to freedom. All aboard!"

The Burners hesitated, looking to me. I nodded. "Get on."

That was all they needed. They rushed aboard. Erin and Bobby carried Kenya and one by one, my friends were on board. We were finally leaving the facility.

The Breathers suddenly realized what was going on.

"You will *not* leave!" Paul yelled. "We will hunt you forever."

No one answered. I was way too exhausted for any witty repartee.

"Laoni!" Redmond yelled, his eyes wide as he took me in. "Get in."

"Is everyone else on?"

"Yeah. Just come on."

I shuffled to the bus. Redmond jumped up and pulled me into his arms, depositing me in the front, next to the driver's seat. I held my fingers up. Ice seemed to drip from every pore in my body. It didn't matter. I had to hold off.

Redmond pulled the door closed and started driving. My ice block stayed…it stayed as he turned onto the road leading out. It stayed as he smashed through the main gate, making the van shudder around us.

Then it faltered.

"Drive as fast as this thing can go. Back to Natalie. Back to the Mountain Lady!" I gasped.

Then, all I could feel was falling. Blackness took me away. Away from the pain. Everything was gone. I think even I was.

CHAPTER 42

Diary, I'm awake now. I had to write. I can't hold the emotions in. Kenya is unconscious. One of the Flyers hit her in the head. Bobby won't stop bleeding. None of us knows first aid. Redmond is concerned with my arm. He thinks it's not set correctly, like he knows anything.

Everyone's asleep except Redmond, who won't tire. They're curled up against each other or the windows. I think the gas is almost out. But we don't dare stop. We're almost there anyway. I'm so tired. I spent so much energy, I can barely hold my head up. The sun in my eyes hurts. It blocks the view of Redmond, my savior.

But we're almost there. Natalie will help us. She'll know where we can go. What we can do. How to heal all of us. I have to believe this. We can't have just escaped from a whole lot of angry Breathers just to die out here, out of gas, losing blood.

I am feeling... Well, do I dare admit it? I feel hopeful. We lost the Breathers. They don't know where we're going and a whole lot of them were injured. I'd bet that they need to regroup, heal a bit, and then look for us. I mean, we struck them a major blow. The facility is in tatters. Their draining machine is destroyed. They lost several of their kind in the last week. And we gave them quite the bloody lip just now.

So, we just need to get to the Mountain Lady, have Natalie call the submarine, and go. Toward the island, toward freedom. And I don't have to worry about leaving anyone behind.

Everything looks rosy. Better than I could have dreamed. I know I am so very tired. I know a few of us are injured. But we're free.

And we're almost there.

It's funny. Burners. There are two kinds. Ice and fire. They have similar powers. They all have energy that can be used to help humans. I can freeze water just by touching it, clothed or not. I can manipulate the ice into forms of my choosing. I still need water, but I have to drink it as slush and it pretty much freezes on the way down. I guess it just adds to my body inside.

I can't swim, bathe, or anything else. I use dry soap and shampoo.

My abilities can't hurt Breathers directly, but I can use the water around me to indirectly attack them. I'm quick and agile. I heal fast. Faster than a normal human, or so I've heard. My cuts vanish in only hours, deeper wounds in days.

Oh, and I'm beautiful. So damned beautiful I cause accidents when people see me. Needless to say, I avoid people. I've looked at myself in reflective surfaces, but I see nothing but my fearful eyes.

I'm also strong. I can lift two hundred pounds deadweight easy. It's like I'm made to fight. I'm born to struggle. And yet all I can do is run.

Oh, and I'm paranoid. Terrified. Angry. Dark. Dangerous.

Ah, Redmond's pointing out the sign toward the Mountain Lady. He's pulling off now. We made it! Diary, we made it! I can't wait for everyone to sleep in those beds. I do hope Natalie has enough. We can probably take turns if not. The wounded first.

The bus is turning the corner now. I see the glimmer of ocean behind...

Oh, shit! No! NO!

It's gone, Diary!

The Mountain Lady is a smoking hole.

I can be as cold as ice. I should have shut down any care about who I left behind. We're all dead anyway.

Humans hate Burners after the initial amazement wears off.

Breathers hunt us.

Burners all die. Always.

CHAPTER 43

I really couldn't speak as Redmond pulled into the new pothole's parking lot and stared at the ruins. The building was gone. The only sign that anything had ever existed there was a shell covered in burnt-out materials. I couldn't even tell there was anything between the ocean and land. It was just gone.

And so was Natalie.

I didn't know what to do. We couldn't all go back to the sewers. Not only was I pretty sure none of my friends would like staying there after having such a great life at the facility, but a lot of us wouldn't survive. The gas sputtered out and the bus died.

"What do we do?" Redmond murmured. He didn't want to wake anyone up. It was too late, though. The lull of the bus was gone and with it the peace that helped the Burners sleep.

"Are we there yet?" Erin asked, blinking, pulling out from under Cindy's sleeping head.

"Just a minute," I barked. I didn't want to move. My legs were lumps of lead. I stumbled and almost fell as I stepped down the bus's stairs and walked forward. I didn't know where I was going. Maybe to the ocean. Maybe into it. But definitely away from the questions. Away from the accusations.

I thought we were safe! I thought you knew what you were doing. I thought you were a hero!

No, I couldn't hear that. I trudged through the ash and dirt, hoping I'd never feel again. I stumbled over the detritus and felt the tears rolling down my cheeks. The tickle irritated me and I wished for the ice that couldn't be felt. I couldn't do this anymore! I was done.

Any hope I had was squashed seconds after having it. Some dark fate was watching over me and tortured me whenever she could. Letting me hope. Letting me believe there was a life for people like me.

I wouldn't hope ever again. I wouldn't give that disgusting jerk a thing.

Even as I thought that, my feet came in contact with something. A form.

Oh no, a body!

I fell to my knees and brushed off the ash.

Natalie!

No!

Then her eyes popped open. "I knew you'd come back. I hid in the ash. It's not so bad, sleeping in ash. Come on, we've got a lot to discuss."

Then I burst into ice. Natalie reached forward and hugged me, ashy fingers and all.

~

I might have been in shock. Natalie was alive. She was more than that—she was ready. She even had some gasoline for the bus hidden away. She asked us to drive away from the remnants of the Mountain Lady Bed and Breakfast and into the shadow of the trees. She let us in on the fact that, though nowhere near as good as water, forests also could mask our presence. It made sense. The facility was surrounded by woods. It kept us secret.

At any rate, we parked on an abandoned road between two lines of trees. Natalie knew a thing or two about first aid, so she bound our wounds with strips of cloth from anyone who had enough fabric on their clothes to spare. We were all very lucky the Breathers had been aiming to wound and not kill. There were no bullets to be yanked out. Not much could be done for Kenya, but Natalie swore there'd be help once the submarine arrived.

Yes, she had already called for it. She had that much faith in us coming back. Or maybe she didn't have any other options but faith.

While the rest of the Burners sat and watched us, wondering what in the world was going on, Natalie told us what had happened.

She had a contact at the facility. One of the humans actually wanted to help us. Not too much, though. They weren't willing to stick their necks out when one of us was murdered.

"We save who we can," Natalie reprimanded. She saw the look I gave when she told me that lovely piece of information. "I get information to her, and she sends stuff back."

That was how Natalie had found out I had been recaptured. But unfortunately for Natalie's Bed and Breakfast and the informant, Digory still had Redmond's scent at the time. He knew the general area where he had lost us, so he watched for anything suspicious at the facility. When a message was intercepted, he told the higher-ups, and they sent a bunch of Flyers to Natalie's. They wanted the complete eradication of anyone who helped.

"There were a lot of humans staying here, but a Breather came in and ordered them all out." Natalie leaned her head against the glass window behind her. The Burners were all crouched up as close as possible on the end where Natalie was. I was afraid the bus might tip over. Redmond was still in the driver's seat, but he was practically twisted in half to stare at Natalie.

She knew stuff that would save us. Without even being told, we all knew that, somewhere in our hearts. Or maybe none of us wanted to give up when we had gotten so far.

"My scent must not be what it used to be," she said with a wry grin. She tugged at her braid and then swung it over her shoulder. "The Breather who came to warn us all thought I was just a collaborator, not one of you."

Dizziness made her head swim before me, but I just shook my head. "So, they destroyed your place."

Her face darkened. Her hand that was rested on the back of the seat tightened into a fist. "My life's work, my home, gone in about thirty seconds. Those Flyers bombed it to the ground. But..." Her smile returned as she took in all our faces. "Thirty-two lives for an old building is a trade I'm more than willing to accept."

I considered that. If we'd had to deal with more Flyers in our escape, we might have lost. Like it or not, the destruction of such a beautiful place allowed us the ability to get on the bus and get out of there.

"So why were you in the ash?"

"I didn't leave. They exploded the place with me inside. I managed an ice shield and just stayed put. I knew you'd be back, so I kept myself hidden in all the ash." Her smile was proud. Well, she had been right. We had come back.

Kenya moaned from her place on Bobby's lap. He had been holding her since she collapsed.

"How much longer before we can meet the submarine?" I asked. "I'm afraid for her."

Her eyes caught mine. She was afraid too. "I sent the message as soon as I could. The submarine was sent out, but it takes hours to get here. It has a stealth mode, but it still needs to make sure nothing is in its vicinity. There are enemy subs that are looking for us too."

I shuddered. Was everyone looking for us? It seemed like every single time we got away, someone else was chasing us. Was there any real peace? Was there any end to this? I didn't want to live this life anymore. I leaned against my own window, leaning my head against the glass, feeling the smooth surface against my scalp. I closed my eyes and felt someone slip next to me. He pulled my legs into his lap. I knew it was Redmond. No one else could feel like him.

His strong voice filled me with strength. "What do we do in the meantime? We all used up a lot of energy. We're starving. There are thirty kids here who just left a war."

"We're not kids," Erin spoke up. "But, yes, we're hungry."

Natalie nodded and grunted under her breath. "Thirty people will raise too much attention in town. But we only have the one vehicle, so we're pretty much stuck here. And all the clothing for Burners ironically enough burned up."

And that was it. We had no food. No warm beds. No special clothing for anyone here. And I just kept getting dizzier. There was nothing to do except wait. This bus wasn't the most comfortable place for us to sit.

But we got through. I ended up just putting my head on Redmond's shoulder and let my mind drift. He held my head to his shoulder and kissed it from time to time.

Suddenly, out of the blue, Natalie nodded. "Okay, the submarine is arriving. Redmond, do you mind if I drive?"

Redmond didn't want to move from my side. "Not at all."

She slid into the seat and we were off again. Driving toward freedom.

"Laoni, are you okay?" Redmond whispered in my ear. I smiled and moved closer so his lips touched mine. He gave me two kisses but repeated his question. It sounded urgent.

"I'm good. I'll be better when we're free."

That was all I said as the bus rumbled back onto the road. Natalie didn't stop driving even when the tires hit the sand. I gazed at the water as I held Redmond's hand. The blue was so beautiful. Such movement and energy. So natural and powerful, but never hated. Not like Burners.

The beach went on for a mile until it reached the side of a cliff. Natalie parked the bus and we all filed out. I waited until everyone was off the bus. I didn't want to move yet. Finally, Redmond stood up and reached his hand out. I took it, and he squeezed.

His eyes burned with concern for me. I couldn't tell why. My ice cast was staying true, and though it ached a lot, I could manage. My ribs already felt better, so I guess they weren't broken. I just needed a place to rest.

At the base of the cliff, there was a little pathway between the rocks that led to an inlet. It was hidden from sight by ocean or land. We all gathered around the edge—Bobby carrying Kenya's unconscious form, which wasn't up to walking—and looked toward Natalie. There was nothing there.

"Just wait," she soothed.

The surface of the water suddenly started bubbling and a golden dome poked out of the surface, followed by a long oval body. The thing was *big*. A hatch was on top that clunked open to reveal a ladder.

Suddenly, a wild head of blonde hair appeared and revealed…

"Natalie?" I asked with shock. This woman looked exactly like her, right down to the same smile.

"No, Nora," the woman said.

"She's my twin sister," Natalie said, enjoying my expression. "I always love this part. Have you got food?" she directed to her twin.

"Food and beds below. Oh, and clothing."

"They keep saying that," Erin muttered. "What's wrong with our clothes?"

I just shook my head. Safety was here. We were on our way.

Nora looked at Kenya. "Oh, come on, boy. Get her inside. We have a little medical room on board. You come, too," she added toward me.

"Me? I'm okay. I've got this." I held up my cast.

"Okay, you'd better carry her," Nora said. I wasn't sure why. Oh, I wasn't actually standing anymore. Somehow, sometime, my legs had stopped supporting me. Everyone climbed down, but Kenya and I were passed down, into the big golden beast underwater.

"What's happening?" I asked once I was in Redmond's arms again and he was walking me down a long narrow passageway with a tight roof. The walls were golden down here.

"Something's wrong, Laoni. Something terrible. With you."

I smiled. "I just have a broken arm. Maybe some bruised ribs." My hand fluttered up to caress his jaw. "We're free."

He brought me to a small white room. Beds stuck out from the side of the wall. There was more than enough space between each bed. Kenya was placed on the far end, and some good-looking doctor started the process of saving her life. I didn't know why I was here. But the bed sure felt good.

"Mond," I said, "are we there yet?"

Mond grabbed my hand and held it. "Almost. Just hold on."

Hold on? I was fine. Nothing was wrong with me. The bleeding had stopped. My arm was in pain, but it seemed very far away. We were safe. I felt the submarine moving through the water. We were headed toward freedom. A place where all Burners were welcome. Where they lived together.

I closed my eyes. It was all over.

CHAPTER 44

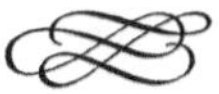

REDMOND

*O*kay Diary,

This isn't exactly your owner. It's Redmond here. I've seen Laoni write in you, and I just wanted to be a part of it. Don't worry, Diary or Laoni, I didn't read any of it. I just wanted to talk to you. Well, not the diary, but to you, Laoni. I'm worried sick. You're unconscious.

There's no reason for it, at least as far as I can see. They've hooked you up to a lot of machines. They say you'll have even better care on the island. When we get there, you won't see our arrival. This is the second time I've watched over your unconscious form, and it doesn't get any easier. I'm afraid, Laoni.

I can't lose you. I never even knew how much I could feel until you touched me that first day. You are my world. You look so beautiful asleep. Your white hair lies like a pillow under your head. Your face is silent. Peaceful.

As much as I love your face when you're asleep, I want you awake more. Awake, you're amazing. Your face, your smile. Your anger. You were like a trapped animal when I met you. Oh, that sounds horrible. I just hate that memory of such unhappiness.

Now, you smile a lot more. I'm arrogant enough to think I had something to do with that.

Laoni, I'm scared. What did they do to you? It's like a portion of you has been drained away.

Laoni, don't go away. You have to read these words someday.

You have to be with me on the island, or who cares about peace? Freedom? All I want is you.

What will I do?

What will I do if you die?

CHAPTER 45

REDMOND

The island was everything Laoni said it'd be. It's not often that I stare in the face of how wrong I was. But these recent events hit me with a two-punch. I had no clue where we had ended up. The entire journey was me watching over Laoni and groaning every time she moaned. When we finally reached the island, I was holding her hand as she was moved. The island is about three miles long. On the north side were lines of buildings where Burners lived in peace. All over the place, there was cultivated land for farming. They had a few animals, lots of fruit trees, and the submarine made a few trips to bring in supplies. The Burners were mainly self-sufficient, though. They couldn't risk exposure by deliveries.

It was warm, but rain came in a lot. Natalie and Nora constantly discussed what to do now that the Mountain Lady was gone and they had no path for new Burners. I didn't join them. I didn't care about saving anyone. I couldn't enjoy the stupid island. The rest of the Burners were thrilled. They were playing in the surf or eating big banquets or making new friends.

I sat, staring at the moving water, remembering when Laoni and I walked the beach for our first real date. It was all I could think of. Kenya was out of danger. She had already healed. But Laoni was still…

I wanted to explode into the air. Leave my body behind. Just become a fireball. If Laoni died… I don't know. I just might do that. That was the question hanging in the air. *If.* She was stable. That's it.

But she wouldn't awaken.

I heard Natalie's steps behind me. Oh, I didn't recognize her steps or anything, I just knew the rest of the Burners stayed away from me. They thought I was a legend who saved them, a downer who was always frowning, or just scary, as I tended to explode these days.

"Unless you're here telling me good news, get lost!" I spat. *Case in point.*

Natalie didn't get lost, and she didn't bring good news. "No change. But I noticed you haven't eaten much."

Try at all. I ignored her.

"But Laoni is going to wake up after we figure out how much damage was done to her. This is new territory. She must have been put into the machine. Drained. But something stopped it."

I knew what. I had saved her. Yay for me. Just a tad too late.

"Blaming yourself is getting you nowhere."

Natalie sounded angry now. Whatever.

"She's going to want a healthy boyfriend when she awakens."

I snorted.

Suddenly, she slapped me! Me! I turned on her with a growl, but then I saw the look on her face. She was worried for me. I couldn't stay angry.

"Natalie, I can't live without her. I never was…positive. I

spent my whole life being angry. But as soon as I met her, I felt hope. I can't have my hope die."

Natalie narrowed her eyes. "She won't die. I don't care what your mind is telling you. Get up. Eat like she'd want you. Do it now."

"But…" I couldn't do as she asked. "My stomach can't… I don't think I can eat. I'm not used to anything but charcoal."

Natalie sighed. "And Laoni's not eating, so you can't."

I didn't answer. I couldn't.

Suddenly, Natalie's head snapped up and she gave a big grin. "Nora!"

Ah, that twin telepathic thing they had. Being both Ice Burners and sisters, they seemed to have extra abilities.

"What?" I asked without interest. The ocean's waves moved onto the beach near my toes and receded again. It was a little rough. Maybe a storm was coming.

"Come on, lover boy. Laoni's awake."

Time moved again. I was aware where I was. My heart flew back to my chest, coming down from the empty misery it was floating on. She was awake!

CHAPTER 46

*T*he island. Belinda told me about it. She told me stories even before we knew there was danger. I always liked her stories.

It is a very lonely island. No other places nearby. Nothing. It is almost like the Bermuda Triangle. Ships are said to have disappeared when nearing the tropical island. It has mounds and mounds of bananas, coconuts, and more. There are lots of people who work together to make a world. All Burners.

Think of that! No humans. No difference. All of us the same. Oops, back to facts. Belinda said there's a little village made of whatever the island could provide. I'm thinking primitive. Wood cabins. No electricity.

There is, at least so Belinda said, a path made up of pebbles embedded in the dirt, and it goes all the way through the village. It splits from time to time to go up to the cabins. Fields of tropical flowers surround the village, coming right up to the cabins and stopping only at the sand line.

The beaches are sandy, and the waters are pristine blue. The sky is cloudy and brings refreshing rain. And Belinda said there *are little farms all over the place where they cultivate food that the island doesn't grow naturally.*

In short, it's paradise. A place for me. A home.

I'm not sure I'll ever get there.

As I fill in this information in my sewer, the last day I'm here, I wonder. What will tomorrow bring?

Will I die before I hit the wonderful shores of Burner paradise?

Only time will tell.

CHAPTER 47

y whole body felt bruised. I had trouble keeping my eyes open, but with every blink, I felt stronger. "Mond, where's Mond?" was the first thing I asked.

"Safe."

That was Nora. My eyes fluttered, taking in light and darkness in equal measure. I think it was Nora. I guess it could have been Natalie. But somehow, I felt it was Nora. Nora didn't have nearly the same motherly feel for me. Not like Natalie, who had comforted me.

"We're all safe."

That wasn't a word I was accustomed to. "Where is he?"

The next words came with amusement. "Aren't you concerned about where you are?"

I blinked again. I finally realized that I was no longer in the submarine hospital. Instead, I was in a wooden house. Lots and lots of wood beams overhead. Like the Mountain Lady, but not the same. That had been destroyed.

"The island?" I asked.

"Better known as Fuego del Hielo."

I gave a grin. "Interesting. But kinda boring in English. Fire of the ice."

Nora laughed. "Let's keep it in Spanish, then. How are you feeling? You've healed, but there's a lot we don't know. Can I ask some questions?"

I pushed myself to sitting. I didn't feel the same dizziness. But there was something more to me. I couldn't put my finger on it. "Shoot."

Before she could continue, my moon barreled into the room. Mond.

"Hey!"

"Hey, yourself," he said, jumping on my bed. I'm glad it wasn't a cot. I think he would have crushed it with his ferocity. I took his hug well. But I felt his pain, his hurt and confusion. How long had I been out?

"Now, now," Nora said. She shot a look at her sister. "Did you have to tell him so soon?"

Natalie waved her away. "He was worried."

"Love is bad for recovering patients."

I leaned into Mond. "Did we make it?" I asked.

"We sure did."

It was almost too much. I knew we had made it to the submarine, but I was so out of it, I never really thought we would succeed. But we had. "Mond, what happens now?"

Natalie fielded that question. "You will leave the hospital and go to your room. It's not much. You don't have your own house."

I laughed. "As long as it's not a sewer, I think I'm happy." I wasn't letting Mond go. He was alternating between stroking my back and kissing my forehead. And I didn't even care that we had an audience.

"We need some answers first." Nora sounded sharp. "The machine. What did it do to you?"

I flashed back to that horrible moment. "It took." I swallowed hard. "I don't know how else to describe it. It took from me. I escaped because of the power outage."

Mond pressed his forehead into my shoulder. He was upset. Probably blamed himself for my own inadequacies.

"What happened to the machine?"

Now that made me smile. "I shredded it with my sweat. I tore it apart."

Nora and Natalie both stared at each other. Lots of thoughts passed between them. Out loud, Natalie said, "That's one benefit. I know that machine is hard to make. There are only three in existence. We can rest for a while. Now, shall we?" Natalie pointed her sister to the door.

"But we have to know more!" she said as her sister pushed her.

"Give them some privacy," Natalie urged.

Mond pulled away and looked at my face. He caressed my jaw and then down the hollow in my neck. "I was afraid for you," he admitted.

"Same," I said back. "But, to quote Erin, I told you so."

That was enough for Mond. He broke into laughter. Then we both started talking at the same time. I wanted to know what had happened since getting to the island. He wanted to know what had happened to me. We got into a rhythm of back-and-forth dialogue all the way into the evening and the next morning. Neither of us wanted to sleep.

Natalie insisted that we go to bed, but after a few hours, we came back together and talked again.

I was having trouble believing where we had ended up. Our fairy tale was ending happily. We had found the island.

It was fantastic too. I felt normal. Mond and I both had rooms in this big dormitory-type building. The other Burners all had their own stories of survival. We had nightly dinners where all sixty of us ate and talked. Nobody was left out. We had nightly games and morning exercises together. We all helped each other to make the island work. The whole thing felt like I was returning to the facility, but in a good way. Family. It was back. And nobody was going to take it away from me again.

EPILOGUE

*D*ear Diary,

It's been a while since I last wrote. I've been too happy. But I have to talk to someone, and Mond won't agree with me.

I overheard Nora and Natalie talking. There are secrets they don't want us to know about. One is me. I was too late to the conversation when I walked the beach one night under Nora's window. Remember, I'm still Strawberry Ribbon, super spy. I heard her say that I was an anomaly. I don't know what that meant. But Natalie very clearly said, "Let's not worry her until we're sure."

I would have confronted them right then, Diary. You know me. I won't let people talk about me without asking why. But the next topic of conversation stopped me.

Diary, there are more facilities out there. More Breathers. More Burners. The ones at the facility weren't the only ones. That little fairy tale Belinda had was a secret code so that Burners could find the peace I have found. But without the Mountain Lady, there's no way they can find us. So many will die.

And it gets worse, Diary, my oldest friend. There are puppet masters behind the puppets. You know what I had wondered, about

Breathers being trapped? It's true. Someone else is out there. They're still gathering Burners, raising them for slaughter.

Natalie is leaving again. She needs to find another way to get the info into the Burners' hands. Otherwise, the puppet masters will get what they want. I'm the only one to have encountered one of those machines and lived.

Diary? I think I'm crazy. I'm going to sneak onto the submarine when Natalie leaves. I'm going with her.

I can't explain it, but let me give it a shot. I've fought my whole life. I've run and been afraid. I know what it's like. I can't leave others to that life, not when I can help them. Staying in peace and happiness on the island would be the same as leaving the facility and my friends so long ago.

I really missed them all! Erin is so much nicer now that she's not filled with conspiracy theories and is just happy. Cindy still worships me, but in a good way. Not the obsessed way she had when we were all trapped.

And the rest of these Burners, all with their tales of terror? I think of them as my brothers and sisters. Somewhere out in the world, more of my family members are being threatened.

I'm going.

~

*D*iary, after all these months, I didn't think I'd write in you so much. But now, I need to turn back to you. I'm on the sub. Natalie didn't notice.

She's exceptionally unobservant. A dangerous flaw in her line of work. Oh, no, it's not because she just didn't notice me sneaking on board. She didn't notice Mond either, who's looking at me with a grin. He was incensed that I would even dream of leaving him behind. He followed me.

And Erin noticed we were going, so she's here too. I wonder if it's because she wants to find her family. And, of course, Bobby is over in the corner.

My whole team. Ready to save the world. Or the Burners. I hear someone coming. We need to get to our hiding places.

～

Natalie isn't unobservant at all.

She came into the empty room and announced. "Okay, be ready. We don't know if there'll be Breathers waiting for us when we rise." Then she left the room. We all slipped out and looked at each other.

It was time.

Look out, Breathers, here we come.

ALTERNATE BURN

books2read.com/burner2

She possesses the chilling power of ice, yet her fate hangs in the balance of a hidden secret...

Laoni, a resilient Burner with the ability to control ice, has faced countless adversaries in her turbulent past, most notably the elusive Breathers—a relentless breed that can sense their prey no matter where they hide. But Laoni has endured something far more sinister: a harrowing encounter with a machine designed to strip Burners of their essence.

Miraculously, she survived, but at what cost? Her body bears the scars of that merciless ordeal, and with each passing moment, her life force wanes. The ice within her, once formidable, now dwindles.

Time is running out, and she must find a way to shield her loved ones from the impending threat of annihilation.

As Breathers grow bolder, a greater menace looms on the horizon—one that sets its sights on her own flesh and blood.

While her love for Redmond burns fervently, Laoni grapples with the cruel reality that her time is slipping away. Releasing him seems inevitable, a sacrifice for his safety amidst the perils that lie ahead. But Redmond refuses to surrender, steadfast in his determination to defy danger and keep her at his side.

ABOUT THE AUTHOR

Marianna Palmer is a creative force who has been crafting captivating stories from the depths of her imagination since she first learned to dream. Encouraged by a dare from her sister, she bravely embarked on a journey into the world of writing, which became her sanctuary during years of solitude, personal challenges, and overcoming deep-rooted fears.

With an unwavering passion for storytelling, Marianna pursued her education and proudly earned her BA degree. However, she didn't stop there. Preferring the enigmatic allure of privacy, she briefly disappeared from the public eye, resurfacing intermittently in the company of her sister before once again retreating into her world of words.

Currently residing in the vibrant city of Tacoma, WA, Marianna draws inspiration from the beauty of her surroundings while reveling in the safety of her sister's presence. Determined to live life to the fullest, she fearlessly confronts the unknown, defying the daunting obstacles that once hindered her path.

https://mariannapalmer.wixsite.com/website

twitter.com/MariannaPalme18
instagram.com/mariannapalmerauthor
tiktok.com/@mpalmerwrites
bookbub.com/authors/marianna-palmer

ABOUT THE PUBLISHER

***VISIT OUR WEBSITE
TO SEE ALL OF OUR HIGH QUALITY BOOKS:***

http://www.redempresspublishing.com

***Quality trade paperbacks, downloads, audio books, and books
in foreign languages in genres such as historical, romance,
mystery, and fantasy.***

www.ingramcontent.com/pod-product-compliance
Lightning Source LLC
Chambersburg PA
CBHW020109310726
48970CB00002B/555